THE BARBARA CARTLAND ETERNAL COLLECTION

The Barbara Cartland Eternal Collection is the unique opportunity to collect all five hundred of the timeless beautiful romantic novels written by the world's most celebrated and enduring romantic author.

Named the Eternal Collection because Barbara's inspiring stories of pure love, just the same as love itself, the books will be published on the internet at the rate of four titles per month until all five hundred are available.

The Eternal Collection, classic pure romance available worldwide for all time .

TEMPTATION OF A TEACHER

Barbara Cartland

Barbara Cartland Ebooks Ltd

This edition © 2019

ISBNs

9781788672191   EPUB

9781788672207   PAPERBACK

Book design by M-Y Books
m-ybooks.co.uk

THE LATE DAME BARBARA CARTLAND

Barbara Cartland, who sadly died in May 2000 at the grand age of ninety eight, remains one of the world's most famous romantic novelists. With worldwide sales of over one billion, her outstanding 723 books have been translated into thirty six different languages, to be enjoyed by readers of romance globally.

Writing her first book 'Jigsaw' at the age of 21, Barbara became an immediate bestseller. Building upon this initial success, she wrote continuously throughout her life, producing bestsellers for an astonishing 76 years. In addition to Barbara Cartland's legion of fans in the UK and across Europe, her books have always been immensely popular in the USA. In 1976 she achieved the unprecedented feat of having books at numbers 1 & 2 in the prestigious B. Dalton Bookseller bestsellers list.

Although she is often referred to as the 'Queen of Romance', Barbara Cartland also wrote several historical biographies, six autobiographies and numerous theatrical plays as well as books on life, love, health and cookery. Becoming one of Britain's most popular media personalities and dressed in her trademark pink, Barbara spoke on radio and television about social and political issues, as well as making many public appearances.

In 1991 she became a Dame of the Order of the British Empire for her contribution to literature and her work for humanitarian and charitable causes.

Known for her glamour, style, and vitality Barbara Cartland became a legend in her own lifetime. Best remembered for her wonderful romantic novels and loved by millions of readers worldwide, her books remain treasured for their heroic heroes, plucky heroines and traditional values. But above all, it was Barbara Cartland's overriding belief in the positive power of love to help, heal and improve the quality of life for everyone that made her truly unique.

AUTHOR'S NOTE

When I visited France in June 1983, I motored with my son to the mountainous fertile Dordogne. Passing along a narrow roadway I saw a magnificent Medieval Château, rising above a small river, very ancient but obviously still inhabited.

We drove closer and found behind it that there was a small attractive village with a lovely twelfth century Church exactly as I have described in this story.

That night we stayed in a very old Château, which had been converted into a hotel. My circular bedroom was in the tower.

It had a beamed ceiling and small windows in a three-foot-thick wall from which there was a panoramic view of the countryside.

Beneath me I was sure that there were dark haunted dungeons!

This story was born before I fell asleep.

Arletta was the name of William the Conqueror's mother, who came from Normandy, and his grandfather, Duke Rollo, had three sons who became Kings of England.

The Granvilles, who are one of the oldest and most famous families in England, can trace their ancestry directly back to Duke Rollo.

CHAPTER ONE
1886

"I am sorry, Lady Arletta. I am afraid it gives you very little time."

"Very little, Mr. Metcalfe."

Lady Arletta Cherrington-Weir gave a deep sigh and her blue eyes were wistful.

Mr. Metcalfe, a precise middle-aged Solicitor, thought that, if it was in his power, he would do anything to sweep away the worried look on her young beautiful face.

He had known Lady Arletta since she was an infant in a perambulator and had watched her grow up, becoming in doing so lovelier year by year.

He thought now that it was impossible for any young woman of twenty to be more enchanting and so completely unselfconscious and unaware of her own attractions.

This, however, was not surprising considering that for the past two years Lady Arletta had been obliged to nurse her father, the Earl of Weir, who had grown month by month increasingly querulous and disagreeable.

He had refused to have anybody else attend to him and treated his daughter, as the doctors and everybody else thought, as he would not have dared to treat a professional nurse.

But nurses were exceedingly difficult to find and in the quiet Counties of England, and especially in the villages, there were no nursing facilities except for the village midwife, who was usually old and fat and reputed to keep herself awake by imbibing large tots of gin through the dark hours of the night.

Arletta therefore had been obliged to nurse her father, who was suffering not only from heart attacks, which gave him excruciating pain, but also from gout, which was entirely due to the large amount of claret and port he insisted on drinking despite the many protests of his physicians.

"If I have to die," he would say angrily, "I may as well have the comfort of feeling drunk and I am damned if I will have the only solace for my disgusting condition taken away from me."

Arletta had long ago given up arguing with him. She merely agreed with everything he said and he then swore at her for being dull and spiritless.

Actually in his better moods he was exceedingly fond of his only child, although it was a bitter disappointment to him that there was no son to inherit the Earldom.

It would therefore pass to his nephew, whom inevitably he disliked.

Arletta did not like Hugo either thinking him a conceited young man who had his own ideas as to how he would run the estate and refused to listen to anything his uncle or she could tell him about it.

Now, two weeks after her father's death, Arletta had been told that her cousin intended to move at once into Weir House and she was to remove herself and her belongings as quickly as possible.

The trouble was, as she had informed Mr. Metcalfe, she did not know where to go.

"You must have some relative you could stay with, my Lady," he queried, "and, of course, if you wish, you can always live in the Dower House."

"I know that," Arletta replied, "and it is very kind of Cousin Hugo to offer it to me. But you know as well as I do, Mr. Metcalfe, that I would not be allowed to live there alone."

She sighed before she went on.

"And I don't think I could bear to see my cousin turn the whole estate upside down and manage it in quite a different way from Papa's methods."

"I am sure you would be wise to go elsewhere," Mr. Metcalfe advised her quietly, "but, because of your father's illness, you were not presented at Court, as you should have been a year ago and you never had the ball, which I know you were looking forward to long before you left the schoolroom."

Arletta smiled.

"I always imagined my ball at Weir House would be a particularly splendid one. Mama used to talk about it when I was quite small and say that it would be the best that the County had ever seen and just like the times when my grandfather was alive."

Mr. Metcalfe was well aware that it was the third Earl who had dissipated the Weir fortune with unbridled extravagance that and plunged the estate heavily into debt.

The late Earl had done his best to develop the land, make the farms pay and ensure that they lived within their means.

But he could not bring back into the family exchequer the revenue from the streets and squares of London that had been sold for what now seemed a pittance and the money that had been squandered by speculating in 'get-rich-quick' schemes that never materialised.

When her father had fallen seriously ill just at the time when Arletta was emerging from the schoolroom, all ideas of entertainment had been set on one side.

As he was extremely disagreeable to those who called to commiserate with him, he and his daughter became more and more isolated in the great house, which seemed unnaturally quiet after years of being filled with guests and a great deal of activity.

Since the Earl could no longer ride, the foxhounds had been taken over by another landowner in the County, the fête, which was one of the great local events of the summer, was held elsewhere and the archery competition no longer took place on their long green lawns.

The whole estate then seemed to be enveloped in a fog of depression and anticipation as to how long the Earl would live.

It was, in point of fact, due to his daughter's care that he had lived longer than expected, but now the end had come and Mr. Metcalfe thought optimistically that it might be a new beginning for Lady Arletta.

"Now, let's think this over sensibly," he said in a business-like voice. "I know all your relatives and I hope you will not think it impertinent of me if I suggest who I think would look after you best and make you happy."

"Of course, dear Mr. Metcalfe, I would be most grateful for any suggestions you can make," Arletta replied. "The trouble is, as you well know, I have very few close relatives living in England."

The Earl's youngest brother, who was actually very much younger than the Earl, was Governor of Khartoum in Sudan and, as he was unmarried, it was not likely that he would want his niece to stay with him in such an isolated and troubled part of the world for any length of time.

Her only aunt, on the other hand, was married to the Governor of the North-West Provinces in India.

As she already had three daughters of her own and found them a problem, Mr. Metcalfe was certain that she would have no wish to have Lady Arletta added to her responsibilities.

There was then a long pause before he said,

"There is, my Lady, your cousin Emily."

Arletta gave a little cry of horror.

"I will not live with Cousin Emily, Mr. Metcalfe! That would be too unkind. You know how she is given to good works and she disapproves of everything such as dancing and singing even if people are happy. I cannot think of anything more depressing than having to live with Cousin Emily!"

Mr. Metcalfe laughed.

"I agree with you, Lady Arletta, so we must think of someone else."

"But who?"

Arletta gave a little sigh before she added,

"I have often wished that I knew some of my grandmother's relatives, but, because they were French, they never seemed to come to England and, although I was named after my grandmother, I have never been to France."

"That is something I had forgotten," Mr. Metcalfe murmured. "Of course 'Arletta' is a French name."

"I have always been told that it was the name of William the Conqueror's mother," Arletta said, "and, because Grandmama came from Normandy, she had fair hair and blue eyes. So although I look English, I also look French."

Mr. Metcalfe laughed.

"I am prepared to believe you, Lady Arletta, although I always think of Frenchwomen as having dark eyes and dark hair."

"Not if they are Normans!" Arletta countered proudly.

Then she went on,

"Unless I am to write to Grandmama's relatives whom I have never seen, who is there in England?"

"There is Lady Travers," Mr. Metcalfe suggested.

Arletta made a little grimace.

Lady Travers was a cousin who in the past had occasionally visited Weir House, but only when she invited herself.

She was the type of middle-aged woman who was always suffering from some strange and unknown complaint that puzzled the doctors. Arletta had decided a long time ago that the only thing that was wrong with her cousin Alice was that she had not enough to do in her life.

She had enough money to live in great comfort, but she had no children and she therefore concentrated entirely on herself and her ailments.

She would spend months in Harrogate and then Cheltenham, until, finding that she was no better in either of these places, she would move on to Bath or just occasionally to some Continental Spa like Baden-Baden or Aix-les-Bains.

Arletta thought that, after two years of coping with one invalid in the shape of her father, it would be utter misery to start all over again with another.

Mr. Metcalfe watching her face knew just what she was thinking.

"Definitely not Lady Travers," he said firmly. "I am trying to remember who else there is."

"That is what I was doing too before you arrived," Arletta admitted, "but I find it hard to believe that in such a distinguished family as ours there are so few of us left."

"There must be somebody," Mr. Metcalfe surmised desperately.

"I have some relatives who live in the very North of Scotland," Arletta answered, "and I believe there is a distant branch of the family in Ireland, but I cannot imagine that they would be very pleased to see me after Papa has ignored them for so long."

As this was palpably true, Mr. Metcalfe did not even trouble to agree with her.

He merely sat doodling on the block in front of him and seeing in his mind's eye the impressive Family Tree that hung in the passage near the library.

Arletta suddenly jumped up from her chair.

"It's no use worrying at the moment," she declared. "I will move my things into the Dower House until I can think of somewhere where I can go."

"You ought to be in London, my Lady," Mr. Metcalfe said. "After all the Season has only just begun and there must be somebody, even though you are in mourning, who would see that you met young people of your own age."

"You say I am in mourning," Arletta replied, "but you will remember that in Papa's will he said expressly that nobody was to wear black, nobody was to mourn for him and the sooner he was dead the better he would be pleased!"

Mr. Metcalfe, who had drawn up the will himself and thought that it was just the sort of thing that the Earl would say, did not reply.

At the time it had seemed rather bad taste and he felt now that spoken in Arletta's soft musical voice it sounded almost cruel.

"No one could have worked harder than you, my Lady," he said quietly, "to make your father happy in the last year of his life and I am well aware of what a difficult patient he was."

"Terrible," Arletta agreed.

Quite unexpectedly she laughed before she went on.

"The doctors could do nothing with him and neither could I. I think the only pleasure he had when he was in such pain was to defy us and do exactly the opposite of what was required of him."

"I am afraid that the late Earl was always a rebel," Mr. Metcalfe sighed.

"And I hope I am one too," Arletta remarked.

Mr. Metcalfe looked at her in surprise and she explained.

"I do *not* intend to be crushed by what has happened to me and I mean somehow, now that I am free, to begin to live."

She did not have to explain to Mr. Metcalfe that, looking after her father in the large, empty dismal house with nobody to talk to, had been to all intents and purposes a living death for a young girl.

"You are quite right," he said aloud, "and somehow in some way you have to enjoy yourself. The first thing I think you should do is to buy yourself some new clothes. My wife always claims that there is nothing like a new gown to cheer herself up."

Lady Arletta gave a spontaneous little laugh that was very attractive.

"I am sure that Mrs. Metcalfe is right," she said, "and that is exactly what I will do. I will go up to London as soon as I have sorted matters out here and, however reprehensible it may seem, I shall buy myself some pretty gowns and, because I know that it would please Papa, they will not be black!"

Mr. Metcalfe picked up his papers that were on the table and put them into a leather bag.

"I think, my Lady," he said, "that is the only sensible thing we have decided upon this afternoon. I promise you I shall think over your problem very carefully and hope eventually to come up with some sort of solution."

He spoke with confidence.

At the same time at the back of his mind he knew that there was really no one who was congenial, understanding and kind in her family who this lovely young girl could appeal to for shelter.

When he said 'goodbye' and Arletta walked with him down the long passages that led to the hall, he thought that the whole house looked dismal and overwhelming and the sooner Lady Arletta was away from it the better.

She had taken on responsibilities this last year that would have seemed heavy and arduous even to a young man and, because he was very fond of her, Mr. Metcalfe wanted desperately to find some magical means by which she could be happy in the future.

'There has to be a way,' he ruminated as he drove away in his ancient pony cart drawn, however, by a young horse, which would make short work of the five miles that lay between Weir House and the small town where he lived and had his office.

When he had gone and Arletta saw him disappearing under the branches of the great oak trees that lined the drive, she walked back into the hall.

She was thinking, as Mr. Metcalfe had done, that the house seemed dismal and even the sunlight could not percolate through the windows to light up the portraits of the many Weir ancestors on the walls.

They needed cleaning and the stair carpet, which was almost threadbare, should have been replaced years ago.

She was well aware that the new Earl would find it all depressing and out of date.

She was quite sure that Cousin Hugo would have very strong ideas of how he could improve the house and had always thought ridiculous the sacrifices that his predecessor had made to restore what had been thrown away in the past.

"A few debts never hurt anyone!" Arletta had heard him say once.

She was sure that he had meant it as a joke.

At the same time she was certain that he did not have her father's strict principles that had made him determined that he would never be in debt even for the smallest amount.

He had also sworn to make good any deficits that his father had left outstanding.

She was intelligent enough to realise that this was the reaction of a man who ever since he was a small boy had known that his father was spending more than he owned and that many people and small firms suffered in consequence.

And yet now it was hard to think that the 'bad old days' might return and she felt that she could not bear after so much pinching and saving to see her cousin Hugo being a spendthrift like her grandfather.

'I must go away,' she told herself firmly.

Slowly she walked back through the hall, where there were no servants, into the room where she had been sitting with Mr. Metcalfe.

It was a very pretty room because, as it faced South, there always seemed to be more sunshine in it than anywhere else and her mother had made it particularly her own.

She had accumulated in it all the furniture that was light, pretty and mostly French and pictures that were quite the opposite of the heavy portraits of the Weirs.

Winter or summer there were always flowers to fill the air with fragrance and make vivid patches of colour against the pale green panelling that had been installed in the reign of Queen Anne.

'I shall miss this room,' Arletta thought to herself.

Instinctively, as if she felt that she would understand, she lifted her eyes to the portrait of her mother that hung over the mantelpiece.

It was a very lovely picture of a very lovely women.

Looking at it, Arletta felt that the smile on her mother's lips and the light in her eyes expressed not only her character and her personality but also her French blood, which made her so different from the Weirs, who could trace their ancestry back to Saxon times.

It seemed strange that her grandfather should have married a Frenchwoman and yet at the same time Arletta could understand that he was a rebel like her father.

His revolt had obviously been against the pomposity of his relations and perhaps too against the heavy atmosphere and gloom of the family house.

'I wish I had known my grandmother,' Arletta had often reflected.

Her mother had said to her,

"You are very like her, my dearest, and when I hear you laugh, I feel like a child again and listening to my mother who always seemed to come into the nursery laughing."

Arletta looked at the portrait for some time and then she said aloud,

"You will have to help me, Mama, because it is going to be very difficult to know what I can do with my life now."

Then she turned away to begin thinking once again that the first real task must be to find herself a chaperone.

She had a vague idea in her mind that there were Ladies of Quality in London who would present a young girl not only at Court but to the Social world.

She had no idea how one began to find one and instinctively, because she was very sensitive, she shied away from pushing herself forward or saying in so many words that she wanted to be noticed.

She also had the uncomfortable feeling that such a plan would suggest that she had the possibility of marriage in mind.

But was she likely to find a husband here in the country where she had lived for so long and where there never seemed to be any eligible bachelors, or if there were, she had never met them.

'I don't want to marry,' she told herself. 'I want to *live*!'

Yet she was aware that in that day and age the two terms were synonymous.

Young women were brought up to get married as quickly as possible after they left the schoolroom.

Nothing else was open to them, the only alternative being to become an old maid, caring for some ill or tiresome parent, as she had done, and then to become a useful aunt to her nephews and nieces.

As she had none, that position was obviously not open to her.

Once again she was back to asking herself the same question.

'What can I do? *What can I do?*'

Then, as she asked it, and it seemed as if even the pictures on the walls were saying the same, the door opened and somebody looked in.

Arletta turned round, stared and then gave an exclamation of astonishment.

"Jane! Is it really you?"

The newcomer, who had just put her head round the door, then came into the room.

"I rang the bell, but nobody answered," she explained. "But I thought perhaps I would find you here."

Arletta ran towards her and kissed her.

"Dear Jane, this is such a surprise!" she enthused. "I had no idea you were at home."

"I arrived only this afternoon," Jane Turner replied, "and, when I heard that your father had died, I came at once to see you."

"That is very kind of you."

"I am so sorry," Jane Turner remarked.

"It was the best thing that could happen," Arletta replied. "His heart attacks grew more frequent and he was in constant terrible pain from his gout. It was only because he was so exceptionally strong that he survived as long as he did."

"Papa told me how well you looked after him," Jane said. "Oh, poor Arletta! It must have been dreadful. I often thought of you."

"It was rather ghastly," Arletta admitted, "but I am so thrilled to see you again, Jane. Why have you come home?"

A smile appeared on the rather plain face of the woman she was talking to, which for the moment made her look almost pretty.

Arletta stared at her and then gave a little cry.

"Something has happened – I know it has! Jane, what is it?"

Jane Turner drew in her breath.

"You will hardly believe it, Arletta, but I am to be married!"

"How wonderful!" Arletta exclaimed. "And to whom?"

"You will never guess," Jane Turner replied. "It is to Simon Sutton!"

For a moment Arletta looked blank.

Then she said,

"You don't mean – it cannot be – ?"

"Yes, it is. You remember him when he was Papa's Curate. You know he went out to Jamaica and in eight years he has risen and risen and, because they appreciate him so much out there, he is to become a Bishop!"

"And you are to marry him!" Arletta cried. "Oh, Jane, how really wonderful!"

"I never thought – I never dreamt," Jane went on, "that he loved me and yet, because he wrote to me almost every week and kept saying how much he missed me, I have, of course, thought about him."

The colour came into her cheeks and she looked down shyly and Arletta put out her hand.

"Oh, Jane, it's like a Fairy story. And he has loved you all this time."

"Ever since he was here in Little Meldon," Jane replied. "I knew in a way that he was unhappy when he left, but I did not dare to think that it was because of me."

"But it was," Arletta insisted.

"Yes. He arrived in England two days ago and told me that now he could afford to be a married man and he wants me to go back with him immediately to Jamaica and to be there when he is consecrated."

Arletta clasped her hands together.

"It's the most exciting thing I have ever heard. Oh, Jane, I am so happy for you and I suppose that you have now come home to be married?"

"Of course. Papa has to marry us," Jane answered, "and, as Simon has something to do in London, he arrives tomorrow evening."

"Dear Jane, I am so very glad that I shall be able to be at your Wedding."

"There is no time to ask many other people," Jane replied, "and, of course, I want you."

She looked a little shy as she asked,

"Will you be my only bridesmaid?"

"Of course I will, Jane, and I should have been very hurt if you had not asked me."

"It seems wrong for me to have one when I am so old. Do you realise I shall be twenty-eight in a month's time?"

"I am sure you are just the right age to be a Bishop's wife," Arletta laughed.

As if she could not help it, Jane laughed as well.

Arletta had known Jane ever since she was a child. Because Jane was the Vicar's daughter, she had not only come to play with Arletta in the Big House, but the Earl had persuaded the Vicar to teach his daughter many of the subjects that were beyond the scope of her Governess.

The Reverend Adolphus Turner was a Classics scholar and Arletta had studied history and literature with him, while the Governess kept to the more mundane subjects.

She was taught music by one teacher and art by another, who both came to their home.

Actually it was Jane, for whom it was planned that she would be a Governess who helped her with a great many other lessons.

Although there was such a difference in their ages, they had become very close friends and, if Arletta loved anyone outside her family, it was Jane.

She was happier now than she could possibly say that Jane was to be married to the man she loved.

It had always seemed to her such a waste that anyone so sweet, kind and understanding could not, because she was not particularly pretty, attract the few local young men who might have been interested in her.

That she was now to be the wife of the Anglican Bishop of Jamaica exceeded all Arletta's hopes and excitedly she made Jane tell her exactly what had happened and what her plans were for the future.

Then Jane commented,

"It seems strange that everything always happens at once."

"What do you mean?"

"Well, I have just been offered what seemed at the time to be a wonderful opportunity and actually I had accepted it."

"What was it?" Arletta asked.

"You remember Lady Langley, who your mother introduced me to when she wanted somebody to teach her children?"

"Yes, of course, I remember."

"Well, I had just finished teaching the last one, who is going to school next term," Jane explained, "when Lady Langley begged me to go to France."

"To France," Arletta exclaimed in surprise.

"It's a very strange story, but Lady Langley's brother married a French girl, the sister of the Duc de Sauterre. Apparently she died four years ago and, although Lady Langley offered to bring up the two children, the Duc insisted that their place was in France."

Arletta was listening intently as Jane continued,

"Because she felt rather remiss at never having visited her niece and nephew, Lady Langley went to the Duc's Château a few weeks ago."

The way Jane spoke made Arletta ask,

"What happened? What was wrong?"

"Well, quite naturally Lady Langley was horrified," Jane said, "because, although David, that is her nephew, is down for Eton and will be going there in a year's time, he cannot speak English!"

"He will have a terrible time, if that is true," Arletta remarked.

"That is what Lady Langley thinks. The little girl, who is younger, is, of course, in the same position, but in her case it is not so urgent."

"So you were going there to teach them?" Arletta said.

"That is what Lady Langley had arranged, and I had promised her that I would leave in what is four days from now."

"Is she very upset that you cannot go?"

"She does not know," Jane answered. "She arranged everything and then she went off with Lord Langley for a cruise in the Mediterranean. It is impossible for me to get in touch with her and I feel dreadful, I do really, Arletta, at letting her down. Equally I can hardly refuse Simon, can I?"

"No, of course not!" Arletta agreed, "but I feel very sorry for the little boy – "

She stopped suddenly.

"Jane!" she said in a strange voice.

"What is it?"

"I think I have found a solution both to your problem and to mine."

Jane just looked at her and after a moment Arletta went on,

"I will go to France in your place! It is what I have always wanted to do and it seems as if Mama has sent you in answer to my prayers!"

Jane stared at her in sheer amazement.

"You cannot do that!"

"Of course I can. Just before you came I had Mr. Metcalfe here and I was worrying myself sick about where I could go and who I could stay with, because Cousin Hugo, whom you will remember, has said that he wants to move in as soon as possible and I am to leave Weir House."

"Oh, Arletta, I am so sorry," Jane said. "It's unkind of him to turn you out of your home, although I suppose you would not really want to stay now."

"No, of course not," Arletta nodded. "But then I cannot live alone in the Dower House nor can I think of any relation who would be pleased to have me to stay."

"I cannot believe that – " Jane began and was then silent.

She knew all Arletta's relations and had always thought secretly that they were a pretty depressing lot.

As if Arletta could read her thoughts, she said,

"You are quite right. That is just what I have been thinking and I am sure, Jane, that I could take your place and be you and nobody need ever know."

"It's impossible!" Jane cried.

"Why?" Arletta asked. "You said that Lady Langley is away on a cruise. For how long?"

"I think at least a month, perhaps six weeks."

Arletta smiled.

"Well, there is no need for her to know what has happened until she returns. By that time I shall have seen France, as I have always longed to do. If I am a success, they will keep me. If not I can come back and perhaps move into the Dower House and pay a companion to live with me."

Jane made a little grimace.

"That sounds really ghastly!"

"I know," Arletta agreed, "but it would be better than staying with one of my aunts or cousins for you know exactly what they are like."

Jane rose from the sofa where they were both sitting and walked across the room.

"I am sure that I am not doing the right thing in letting you go to France," she stated bluntly.

"What do you mean?" Arletta asked.

There was a little pause as Jane was obviously choosing her words rather carefully.

Then after a moment she responded,

"Lady Langley told me that the Duc was a very fierce and rather terrifying person. Actually I am not worried about him so much as the other Frenchmen you will meet for, Arletta, you are very very pretty!"

Arletta laughed.

"Now I know what you are thinking about, but it is very unlikely that any Frenchman, who I have always been told are excessively proud and give themselves great airs, would take notice of a mere Governess."

Jane, knowing how innocent Arletta was, wondered how she could put into words what the Frenchmen were likely to think about a Governess who was quite as pretty as her dear friend.

Then she remembered that Lady Langley had been almost apologetic in asking her to undertake the education of her nephew and niece because the Duc's Château was in such an isolated part of the Dordogne.

There were, she had said, no companions for Pauline and David because, as far as she could ascertain, there were very few neighbours in the vicinity of the Château.

"The Duc spends most of his time in Paris, which is a good thing, because as far as I can make out, he terrifies the whole staff of the Château, which is a splendid example of French architecture and is kept up in a magnificent almost Royal manner."

She paused and knew that Arletta was listening intently before she continued.

"Lady Langley went on to say, 'I am afraid, dear Miss Turner, you will find it very dull, but I am so distressed that my nephew will suffer at Eton simply because the Duc has a most unfair prejudice against the English!'

"'He has?' I asked her in surprise.'

"'He was very angry when my brother, Richard, married his sister and so were his father and mother. But they fell in love and to all intents and purposes eloped together. When it was too late for her parents to do anything about it, they went back and said that they were sorry to have upset them and they were forgiven. But according to reports the present Duc never forgave his sister. Not even when Richard died and was followed a few years later by her.'

"'It sounds like a novelette, I commented.'

"'I suppose it does really,' Lady Langley said apologetically, 'but the children are going to suffer and that is something I cannot allow.'

"'So you have persuaded the Duc to employ an English Governess? I answered.'

"'I can assure you that he is very reluctant to do so and says he has no wish to have an Englishwoman inside his house,' Lady Langley replied.'

"'But you managed to persuade him!'

"'With great difficulty and I am afraid, Miss Turner, in consequence, you will not have a very warm welcome. But will you please, and I do beg of you, almost on my knees, do this for my sake?'

"I could hear the beseeching note in the voice of the employer who had been exceedingly kind to me in the six years I had taught her children, so you can understand that after that, I could hardly say no."

"Of course you could not," Arletta agreed, "and it would be terrible to let her down now she is so happy to think that the boy at any rate will be able to speak English."

She knew that Jane was hesitating and added,

"It's a question of time as far as he is concerned and, if you refuse to teach him and do not send anyone in your place, the Duc will be more prejudiced against the English than he is already. David will therefore arrive at Eton speaking only French, which will be disastrous!"

"I must say," Jane said, "although my conscience was pricking me and I was feeling very uncomfortable, I never thought of finding someone to send in my place."

"If you are now thinking of looking around for another Governess," Arletta suggested, "you are much mistaken! I intend to go instead of you. Honestly, dearest Jane, it's the answer I have been waiting for and is like a sign from Heaven that I am not forgotten."

Jane gave a tender little laugh.

Then she declared,

"No one could ever forget you, Arletta. You are the nicest person I have ever known and you know that Papa and I and everybody else in the village love you."

"Thank you. If you love me, then let me do what I want to do and that is to go to France."

She gave a cry and then went on,

"Just before you arrived I was looking at Mama's portrait for signs of her French blood."

"I cannot imagine anybody could look more English than your mother," Jane remarked, glancing up at the portrait.

"That is where you are wrong for she was Norman. My grandmother came from Normandy and Mama told me that all her relatives had blue eyes and fair hair."

Jane did not speak for a moment and then she suggested,

"Perhaps it would please the Duc to know that you had French blood in your veins. On the other hand it might make him feel that you are not such a good teacher of English as you might otherwise be."

Arletta laughed.

"Now you are trying to frighten me, but I can promise you, Jane, that I am not in the least afraid of the big bad Duc! If he is too ferocious, I can always come home without a reference. To go there will not alter my future life as it would yours."

Jane put her arm around Arletta's shoulders before she said,

"If I let you go, Arletta, will you give me your solemn promise, and I mean this very seriously – "

"What is it?"

"That you will not listen to anything flattering or complimentary that is said to you by any Frenchman."

"Why should you say that?"

"Frenchmen are different from Englishmen. First of all they are married when they are very young, as I understand the Duc was, obeying the choice of their parents. It is not a question of love but of convenience."

"Mama told me about this," Arletta remarked. "It sounds to me a very cold-blooded way of getting married."

"I am sure it is, but it is something that happens and after that they usually have a great number of love affairs, which, of course, Papa would think very reprehensible."

Arletta was silent before she answered,

"I don't think it is peculiar to the French. After all, even here in Little Meldon, I have heard people talking about the love affairs of the Prince of Wales."

"They should not gossip to you about his behaviour," Jane said sharply.

Arletta laughed.

"You cannot shut me up in a glass case, dear Jane, even though you have always tried to keep everything unpleasant from me ever since I was a baby."

Jane smiled.

"You were such an adorable child, just as you are adorable now. It seems wrong somehow that you should ever hear about anything that is distasteful and nasty in life."

"While you can, I suppose," Arletta laughed. "Oh, Jane, I have grown up now. I am nearly twenty and, although I do live, as one might say, in the back of beyond, I read the newspapers and novels. It was in fact the main recreation I had when Papa was ill and I had to look after him. My only other relaxation was when I gossiped with the servants."

Jane chuckled.

"I am sure it has been a life of scintillating amusement!"

Then, because she thought that she had been too frivolous, she went on.

"Dearest, I know the terrible time you have had. Papa has told me about it. If it will really make you happy to go to France and as long as you promise to take the greatest care of yourself, I will agree, even though I think it wrong for me to let you do so."

"You really will?" Arletta pressed her excitedly.

Her eyes were sparkling and she looked so lovely that Jane thought that everybody would tell her that it was crazy for anyone looking like Arletta to even think of going off to France and having no idea of what might happen to her there.

"I shall have to think about it," she said.

"There is nothing to think about," Arletta insisted, "except how I can be you. I suppose, Jane, you have a passport?"

"As a matter of fact I had one ready, but now I shall not need it because Simon is arranging for me to be included on his as his wife."

"Well, that solves one problem," Arletta observed. "I shall be 'Miss Jane Turner'!"

"It does not suit you?"

"It suits me far better than you think," Arletta argued. "I shall be Miss Jane Turner, off to France to see the world!"

"I think you are going to find it a very small one. Just a Château in a very quiet isolated part of the country with two children and a great number of servants. I doubt if there will be anybody else."

"I shall be very disappointed if I do not see the disagreeable Duc!"

"If you do, you must promise to look severely business-like and make it quite clear that you are a Vicar's daughter."

Jane paused and then she added,

"Promise me that you will always, always lock your bedroom door at night!"

Arletta stared at her for a moment.

And then she went into peals of laughter.

"Oh, Jane," she giggled. "You have been reading far too many novels! I don't believe for a moment that the grand, stuck-up proud Duc will condescend to notice a poor, humble little Governess and if, as you say, he is always in Paris, he is doubtless surrounded by all the beautiful exotic women who any real lady pretends do not exist!"

"And you are a real lady, Arletta," Jane said.

"But not so stupid or so half-witted as not to know that the *courtesans* of Paris are the most extravagant, the most exotic and the most seductive women in the whole world!"

Jane looked at her severely.

"You should not be talking of such things and how dare you even know of the existence of such terrible women?"

"I have read about them, heard about them and, if you want to know, occasionally Papa has talked about them," Arletta retorted. "Really, Jane, if anyone is being a fuddy-duddy with her head buried in the sand, it's *you!*"

Jane threw up her hands as if in dismay and Arletta laughed.

Her laughter seemed to lighten the room as if sunshine was suddenly flooding into it.

CHAPTER TWO

As the ferry was steaming towards Bordeaux, Arletta thought this was the most exciting thing that had ever happened to her.

She had had a dozen arguments with Jane before she finally capitulated and agreed that Arletta should go to France.

"Remember, dearest Jane," she said over and over again, "that I can come home if things do not go right for it does not matter to me if I don't have a reference as it would have to you."

Jane saw the logic of this.

At the same time she was desperately afraid that Arletta, innocent and completely without knowledge of the world, would find herself in difficulties that she would not be able to cope with.

But she was reassured by everything that Lady Langley had told her about the Duc de Sauterre and also, as Arletta herself had said, she could always come home if she wanted to.

"Anything," Arletta emphasised fervently, "would be better than settling down in the Dower House or being forced even for a little while to live with one of my relations."

She had discussed with Jane the possibility of her finding someone who could chaperone her in London and present her at Court.

Jane said at once that the person who would be best able to help her there would be Lady Langley.

"As soon as she comes back from her cruise, you must talk to her about it," she added, "and I am sure, as you have taken my place with her nephew and niece, she will feel very grateful and under an obligation to you."

Arletta knew that Jane was right and that Lady Langley, who had been a friend of her mother's, would most certainly help.

She had been kindness itself when her father had written to her on Jane's behalf asking her if she could recommend her as a Governess.

Lady Langley had written back saying that she was in need of a Governess for her own children and she was sure that anyone who had lived in their village and was known to them would be very suitable.

Jane had in fact been a great success as Governess to Lady Langley's children and as she said she had been very depressed at the thought of leaving the house where she had been so happy.

"Lady Langley is just like your mother," she told Arletta, "and I know that, just as she looked after me, she would be only too willing to look after you."

"All I have to do," Arletta said, her eyes dancing, "is to fill in the time until Lady Langley returns from the Mediterranean and what could be better than that I should do so teaching her nephew and niece. And, of course, seeing France, as I am longing to?"

Finally Jane was convinced and she showed Arletta the instructions that she had received from the Duc's secretary.

He had written in a rather stiff ponderous English, very obviously translating it, and Jane commented,

"I don't know whether I should be insulted that he thinks I would not understand French."

Then she laughed,

"One thing is quite certain that you speak French, Arletta, better than I do, in fact like a native."

"Which I am because of my Grandmama."

Her mother had been so insistent that she should speak the Parisian French as spoken by the great families of France, that they had often had 'French Days' when Arletta was small when they spoke nothing but French whatever they were doing.

It became a game that even her father joined in with and Arletta knew that by the time her mother died her French was perfect.

It was certainly going to come in very useful now and, as the ship carried her towards Bordeaux, she practised sentences to herself and read a French novel that she found amongst her mother's books.

The sun was shining and Bordeaux from the sea looked very inviting despite the fact that Arletta knew that it had always been a commercial town.

Since the time of the Romans it had become a leading centre of the wine trade and Arletta thought that her father would have been interested if he knew where she was for it was the red wine of that area that had made him suffer so acutely in the last years of his life.

The instructions that Jane had given her told her that, when the ship arrived at Bordeaux, she was to take a train that would bring her to the Station nearest to the Duc's Château and there she would be met by a carriage.

Everything was very clear and the only trouble was that the ferry had been late in leaving Plymouth Harbour and therefore they were late in docking.

Although if punctual, she would have had several hours before catching the train, Arletta was very afraid that she might miss it.

She had never before travelled by herself and she was surprised at how many people offered to help her.

The porters had vied with each other to carry her baggage, several elderly women asked if there was anything she needed and she had no idea it was because she looked so lovely and at the same time so young and helpless.

She and Jane had had a long talk over what she should wear as a Governess in the Duc's Château.

"I have not bought anything while Papa has been so ill, so everything I possess is really in rags," Arletta pointed out. "And so I must have some new gowns and I was going to buy a whole new wardrobe of clothes in London."

"You must certainly not have anything too smart," Jane told her firmly, "or I am sure that the Duc will be suspicious that you are not what you appear to be."

"But I have no wish to look like a beggar-maid," Arletta replied, "and I think in what I am wearing now even the children would question my authority."

Jane ruminated that it was not her clothes that would make them question her but her looks, but there was no point in saying so and starting the argument all over again as to whether she should or should not go.

She therefore suggested,

"The best thing we can do is to go into Worcester. You can buy some clothes there that will not look too sensational or expensive to be beyond the purse of an ordinary Governess."

They left the next morning very early so that they could be back at the Vicarage by the time Simon Sutton was due to arrive.

As Jane had known, there were some very pretty clothes in the shops of Worcester, as it was a large Market town.

She had, however, to admit to herself that whatever Arletta put on seemed to become a perfect frame for her beauty.

She also had a way of wearing her clothes that gave her a style of her own, which again Jane without saying so thought was due to her French blood.

'She has *chic*,' Jane told herself, 'which is something I could never acquire.'

She was very touched when Arletta insisted on buying her a dress and a coat to travel to Jamaica in and a very pretty evening gown as well.

"It is part of my Wedding present to you," she insisted, "and will be far more useful than a brooch or a necklace, which I would have given you otherwise."

"You are not to be so extravagant," Jane scolded her automatically.

"If that is the repressive voice you use to your pupils, then I am sorry for them," Arletta countered.

Then they were both laughing and buying clothes seemed to be so amusing too until they returned to the Vicarage feeling that the whole day had been one of sunshine.

Simon Sutton was waiting for them and, when Arletta saw the expression in his eyes when he looked at Jane, she realised how lucky Jane was.

It did not matter to him that she was actually rather plain. He loved her and there was no doubt that Jane was head over heels in love with the only man who had ever wanted to marry her.

*

At their marriage, which took place the following morning, Arletta was sure that the angels were joining in with the choir and singing a glorious hymn of praise.

No bride or bridegroom ever looked more radiant than Jane and Simon when they walked down the aisle together.

Arletta had remembered at the last moment where her mother had put away the exquisite lace veil that had been worn for generations by the Weir brides.

She insisted on Jane wearing it, together with a small diamond tiara that was also a family heirloom, but which she thought privately Cousin Hugo would consider not large enough to be impressive.

The big tiaras, the necklaces, the bracelets and the brooches that had all been part of the family treasures had been sold by her father as soon as he had inherited to meet her grandfather's debts.

He had, however, kept only this one small tiara for her mother to wear on special occasions.

Although Arletta had often looked at the portraits of the previous Countesses, glittering like Christmas trees, and regretted that their jewels were no longer there, her mother had merely laughed.

"I am quite happy as I am," she had said, "and I can assure you, darling, that peace of mind is a far better ornamentation than a load of unpaid debts."

Anyway Jane was thrilled with being lent anything so beautiful and Arletta knew that the fact that she looked, as she put it 'a real bride' in Simon's eyes, made her Wedding even happier than it was already.

There were only a few guests to drink the health of the bride and bridegroom and they set off to have a few days honeymoon alone before they finally left for Jamaica.

Jane hugged Arletta when she said 'goodbye' to her and whispered,

"Promise me you will look after yourself. I shall worry about you and will pray that you will be safe."

"Of course I will be safe!" Arletta asserted. "If anything goes wrong, I shall just tell the Duc what I think of him and come home. After all, if I am in any difficulty, I know that your father will look after me."

"Of course he will," Jane replied, "but I have not told him what you are doing."

"No one must know, because if they do, they will try to stop me."

Jane kissed her again and then hurried to where her husband was waiting for her.

*

Arletta went back to the Big House to write only one letter before she left three days later.

This was to Mr. Metcalfe.

She told him that she was going to France to stay with some friends and gave him the address of the Duc's Château, just in case it was imperative for him to get in touch with her.

She was so busy her last days at home packing up that she hardly had time to think of what lay ahead of her.

She knew that once she had left it might be very difficult to have anything she wanted without having to plead for it with her cousin, which she would dislike having to do.

She therefore ordered the gardeners and the other servants to move to the Dower House everything that she particularly wished to keep that had belonged to her mother and found it quite surprising how much there was.

There was furniture, books, pictures and what she had forgotten was that the old housekeeper had kept all her mother's clothes carefully put away in wardrobes in the attics at the top of the house.

She used to go over them regularly in case they were eaten by moths.

Because Arletta had been so unhappy at her mother's death and then almost before she had recovered from it her father began to be ill, she had never given a thought to her mother's furs and her other clothes that she had always looked so lovely in.

Now, although many of them were out of date, she thought that some of the dresses would certainly suit her and could be altered, while the furs and coats would be useful in the winter.

"Why did you not remind me that we had all these clothes?" she asked the housekeeper.

"I thought it might bring back unhappy memories, my Lady," was the answer and there was no reply to that.

Because they in fact brought back memories of happier days, Arletta put some of the items that had belonged to her mother into the luggage she was taking with her to France.

There were some beautiful nightgowns and to wear over them a negligée of blue satin that was far more attractive than the plain wool of the dressing gown that Arletta had worn since she was sixteen.

'No one will see me,' she told herself, 'so I shall look glamorous when I am alone at night – and what could be more appropriate in a Château?'

However much Jane had disparaged the Duc by repeating what Lady Langley had told her, Arletta could not help thinking that it would be rather like living in a Fairytale.

She was going to an enchanted Château in France in an area that she knew from her books was famous for its ancient Châteaux.

She wished that she had had more time to read about the Dordogne where the Duc's family had lived for centuries.

Of course, when she wanted them she could not find any books about that particular part of France and thought that the first thing she would do when she had time was to try to find guide books that would tell her all she wished to know.

When she reached Bordeaux, she found herself thrilled and delighted with the people she could see in the streets, largely because they looked so different from anyone in England.

The ordinary peasants with their full skirts and shawls over their heads had a charm of their own, as had the nuns with their varying headdresses.

There was also occasionally a glimpse of women dressed in the strange lace cap and lace-trimmed apron that was characteristic of the district and even the *Gendarmes* in their smart uniforms looked as if they had stepped straight out of an operetta or a musical comedy.

There was, however, little time to look round on her way to the Station and she actually caught the train with only ten minutes to spare.

She watched from the window the undulating countryside, the huge woods that seemed to her like dragon forests and an occasional glimpse on the top of a hill of an ancient Château.

This, Arletta told herself, was Fairyland as she had always wanted to see it.

Her first glimpse of the Duc's Château was exactly what she had hoped it would be.

Silhouetted against the sky it looked very impressive, very formidable and, although she would hate to admit it, rather intimidating.

In the distance the windows seemed little more than arrow slits and the crenelated tops of some of the towers reminded her of the soldiers who must have once guarded the Château and been ready to repel enemies from whatever direction they came.

Beneath the Château there was a river and a stone wall rose straight above the bank on one side to where the building itself began.

Arletta found herself thinking of dark dungeons where prisoners were incarcerated in damp darkness until they died and, as they drew nearer, she had the uncomfortable feeling that eyes were watching her from the narrow windows.

Then, as the carriage that had met her at the Station crossed a bridge and passed the Château, she realised that they were approaching it from the East side and were now moving up a narrow roadway with cottages on either side of it.

Almost at the top was a very ancient Church, which Arletta felt certain was twelfth century like the Château.

Then there was a double gate in the centre of the great wall that led into the Château itself.

She drew in her breath as they drove into a great courtyard at the far end of which there was the impressive entrance to the Château up a large number of steps with an arched doorway, romantically carved and yet rather severe and again somewhat foreboding.

The carriage, which was drawn by four horses, came to a standstill and a footman wearing an elaborate claret-coloured livery trimmed with gold braid ran down the steps to open the door.

Arletta stepped out and she thought that he looked at her in surprise.

Then at the top of the stairs there was an even more imposing figure, who she guessed was the Major Domo.

"You are Mademoiselle Turner?" he asked her in French.

"Yes, that is right."

"Please come this way, *m'mselle.*"

He led her through what she felt was an extremely impressive Medieval hall with a huge open fireplace that could easily burn a whole tree in the winter.

There were ancient flags hanging on either side of it, but she had only a quick glimpse before the Major Domo escorted her down a long passage.

She wondered where she was being taken until he opened the door of what she guessed immediately was the office of the secretary, saying as he did so,

"Mademoiselle Turner has arrived, *monsieur.*"

A middle-aged man with greying hair rose slowly from behind a desk and Arletta knew that this would be Monsieur Byien, who had written to Jane and given her all the necessary instructions for the journey.

He held out his hand and then, as he looked at Arletta, the smile on his lips seemed suddenly frozen and he stared at her in astonishment.

"You are Mademoiselle Turner?"

It was a question.

"I must thank you, *monsieur,*" Arletta replied to him in her perfect French, "for the excellent directions you gave me for my journey. The ferry was a little late arriving at Bordeaux and I was afraid that I might miss the connecting train, but, as you see, I am here!"

"Will you sit down, *mademoiselle*?"

Monsieur Byien indicated a chair in front of the desk and Arletta sat down, wondering if perhaps she should have worn spectacles to make herself look older and academic.

She had actually considered it and then thought that it seemed a theatrical gesture that she might regret.

Also she was quite certain that sooner or later she would forget the spectacles and everybody would be aware that she could see without them.

Instead she had arranged her hair in a very plain and what she hoped was an unattractive way and wore a bonnet that had belonged to her mother and was far too old for her.

Her efforts had obviously not been very effective as Monsieur Byien then remarked,

"I understood from Lady Langley, *mademoiselle*, that you are very much older than you look."

"I have always been told, *monsieur*, that it is rude for a gentleman to discuss a lady's age and, if I look young, which I take as a compliment, it is something that I assure you will be remedied by time."

Monsieur Byien smiled and it swept what Arletta realised now was a look of anxiety from his lined face.

"That is indisputable, *mademoiselle*," he said. "But you must forgive me when I say that I was not expecting an English Governess to look like you."

"Let me reassure you, *monsieur*," Arletta responded, "that I am a very good Teacher of English, which I understand is why I am wanted here. I cannot believe that my looks, one way or another, will affect my proficiency in my own language."

"English may be your own language, *mademoiselle*," Monsieur Byien remarked, "but I must compliment you on your French."

"Thank you," Arletta nodded, "and, if you think my French is good, I assure you that my English is very much better!"

"Then, as you say, that is all that matters," Monsieur Byien smiled.

But again he looked worried and Arletta was aware that there was something about her appearance that he did not mention, but was certainly, from his point of view, a distinct disadvantage.

He rose to his feet.

"I am sure, *mademoiselle*, that you would like to see your rooms and meet your charges and I feel sure that they are looking forward to meeting you."

He led Arletta from his office for what seemed a long walk along the ground floor of the Château.

It certainly was palatial, the furniture naturally being of a much later date than the Château itself.

There was, because the windows were so small, little light and Arletta had the idea that in the winter and when it was dark the shadows would be oppressive and rather frightening.

They climbed a staircase, which was obviously not the main one of the Château, to the next floor and, as they entered the room at the top of it, Arletta realised that they were in one of the round towers.

The room was a sitting room or rather, she guessed, the schoolroom and there were two children in it.

On a table the boy was arranging a number of toy soldiers that were skilfully made of wood and painted,

The small girl was watching him, holding a doll in her arms as she did so.

They both looked up as Monsieur Byien entered and their eyes went from him straight to Arletta.

"Mademoiselle Turner has arrived," he told them in French, "and I know you have been looking forward to meeting her."

He walked to the table saying,

"This, *mademoiselle*, is David, who as you see has a fine collection of soldiers, and this is Pauline."

Arletta held out her hand.

"I am delighted to meet you, David," she began, "and I hope you will show me all your soldiers. My father had a collection of them that he was very proud of."

She was just about to say that, when they were set out, they depicted the Battle of Waterloo, but then she thought that it would be somewhat tactless in a French household and turned instead towards Pauline.

The little girl had curly chestnut hair falling on either side of a very sweet pretty face that seemed filled with two large eyes.

"Do we have to do lots and lots of lessons, *mademoiselle*?" she asked.

"I hope not," Arletta replied to her, "but I certainly want you to tell me all about this magnificent Château and, since I want to learn all about it, that will be a lesson for me."

The two children looked at her in surprise and then Monsieur Byien said,

"Your rooms, *mademoiselle*, like the children's, are on the floor above and when you are ready I am sure that Pauline will show you the way upstairs."

"Thank you," Arletta smiled.

He looked at her again, she thought, with a worried expression on his face before he went from the schoolroom closing the door behind him.

Arletta slipped off her travelling cape, which had made her feel rather hot for the last part of the journey, untied the ribbons on her bonnet and put them down on a chair by the door.

Then she turned to the children,

"I expect you know that I have come here to teach you English, but you must tell me how it would be best for me to do so, because you, David, have to learn the language very quickly."

David looked down at the soldiers that he was holding in his hand and said,

"I want to learn English and then I can go to England and never come back here again!"

He spoke violently and then looked over his shoulder towards the door as if afraid that he had been overheard.

Arletta was surprised.

And then she enquired,

"Are you saying that you do *not* like living here at the Château?"

David was silent for a moment and then, as if he saw no reason why he should tell the truth, he exclaimed,

"I hate it! I am English, I am not French! They are our enemies!"

As he spoke, he gave another quick look over his shoulder and Arletta said,

"They are not our enemies now. England is friendly with France, but, of course, you are English. Have you ever been to England?"

David shook his head.

"No, but *mon père* used to talk about England and he told me that one day I would live there, but Uncle Etienne wants me to stay here."

He lowered his voice before he went on,

"He is hoping that I shall be sent away from Eton as soon as I get there. But, if I cannot stay there, I shall run away and hide somewhere in England so that I shall not have to come back to France."

The way he spoke told Arletta that there was a distinct problem here that she had not expected.

Then, when she was wondering what she should say next, the door opened and a servant appeared carrying a tray.

"The chef's compliments, *m'mselle* and he has ordered you English tea. We don't have such a thing in the Château, but he said bein' English you would expect it. But we do have a little China tea."

"Thank you very much," Arletta replied. "After a long journey a cup of tea is what I would really enjoy."

The servant put the tray down on a table and she saw that it contained a pot of tea, a cup and two plates, one full of sandwiches, the other with little *patisseries* filled with cream that only the French could make so skilfully.

As soon as the servant had left the room, both the children ran towards the table to stare at the tea with curiosity.

"I remember my father having tea like this," David said, "but we are not allowed tea here. We have to be French and drink coffee or wine."

"I expect you would like to share my tea with me," Arletta suggested. "Suppose you both start with a sandwich?"

The children ate most of the sandwiches and enjoyed the *patisseries* as well.

Pauline said very little until, licking the cream from her fingers, she asked Arletta,

"When David goes to school in England, may I come and live with you?"

"When David comes to England, you will live with your aunt," Arletta answered. "I feel sure that she would like to have you."

"Uncle Etienne hates her!" Pauline replied. "So if I am to live in England, I will have to hide somewhere where he will never find me!"

Arletta could not say that this was untrue and she therefore said after a long pause,

"You will have to tell me why your uncle hates England so much."

"He hates everybody and everything," David piped up, "but we are too frightened of him to say so."

"It would be very rude if you did, as you are living in his house," Arletta remarked.

"He hates us too!" David said in a low conspiratorial voice. "But rather than let us go, Uncle Etienne will shut us up in the dungeons!"

The way he spoke made Arletta laugh.

"I am sure that is not right. Nobody is shut up in dungeons these days."

"Uncle Etienne would use them if he could," David insisted. "I will show them to you and you will see the bones of the prisoners who died there."

Arletta shuddered.

"I have no wish to do that. Now suppose you both show me my bedroom and where you sleep?"

There was a twisting stone staircase on one side of the tower only just wide enough, Arletta thought, for the servants to carry her trunks up to her room.

As she reached it, she felt very high up in the air and isolated almost from the world.

The children had two rooms, each occupying half of the floor above the schoolroom and she was on the floor above them.

Her bedroom had windows on each side, which gave her a magnificent view of the surrounding countryside and the room itself had a very high ceiling with ancient beams that were carved and the space between them was painted red.

The carpet was the same colour and so were the short curtains over the windows.

Above her bed there was a strange Heraldic design and David explained it to her,

"This was the room used by one of Uncle Etienne's ancestors who fought against the English and killed twenty men before he himself was struck down."

There was a little pause before he added almost as if he felt as if he should not do so,

"The servants say he haunts the whole tower, but actually the Château is full of ghosts!"

"Is it really?" Arletta asked him. "Have you ever seen one yourself?"

"I have!" Pauline chimed in. "I have seen lots and lots of ghosts and, although the servants run away and scream, I am very brave. I just say a little prayer, like Mama taught me to do, and they disappear."

"I expect that they were only shadows," David said scornfully. "The real ghosts in the Château are not what you see but what you hear, prisoners groaning, the wounded crying out in pain and the shrieks of those who are being stabbed to death!"

He spoke so dramatically that Arletta gave a cry.

"You are not to frighten me. And I am sure if you talk like that you will frighten your sister."

David shrugged his shoulders in a gesture that was typically French.

"We have to put up with it, whatever we feel," he moaned. "If you want the truth, *mademoiselle*, I don't believe we will ever escape and be able to get to England."

"That is nonsense," Arletta responded to this quickly. "In a year's time you are going to Eton, which as you know, is the best school in England and that is why your uncle has been persuaded by your aunt, Lady Langley, to allow me to come here to teach you English."

She paused to add impressively,

"But you will have to work hard, because you would hate being the only boy in the school unable to speak to all the others. So the sooner we start the better."

"I want to learn," David insisted, "not because I am going to Eton, because I am quite certain that Uncle Etienne will stop me from doing that, but so that I can escape. I have – "

He had started to say something and then he stopped as if he thought that it would be indiscreet to tell her his secrets and walked away abruptly to gaze through the window.

Arletta looked round and saw that the servants had brought up her trunks and opened them for her and, while she was wondering if she should unpack and perhaps ask the children to help her, a maidservant in a mobcap came into the room and bobbed a small curtsey.

"The housekeeper says I'm to unpack for you, *m'mselle.*"

"That would be very kind," Arletta replied. "I hope there will be room for all my clothes."

"I'll find room," the maidservant replied confidently.

Arletta looked at the watch that had belonged to her mother and which was pinned on her blouse.

"It's nearly six o'clock," she said to the children. "You must tell me what you do and at what time you go to bed."

"We have dinner downstairs in the dining room at seven o'clock," David answered.

"In the dining room?" Arletta repeated in surprise.

"Uncle Etienne said French families eat together and children eat at the same time as their parents. It is only the

English who send their children to bed because they don't like the sight of them!"

"That is not true," Arletta asserted rapidly. "English children are sent to bed early because being young they need more sleep than grown-ups."

"Uncle Etienne says only the French behave with affection to all their relations from grandparents down to the youngest child. But English children are shut away in the nursery or in the schoolroom until they are grown up because their parents and everybody else think they are bores."

There was some truth in this Arletta had to admit, but she thought that it was extremely unfair of the Duc to use it as a weapon to try to put his nephew and niece against their father's people.

Aloud she said,

"I have plenty of arguments in defence of the English, but I think, as I am rather tired, that I would like to wash now and change my gown and I will join you later. Then you can show me where we have dinner."

"Very well," David agreed. "We will say *au revoir, mademoiselle.*"

He bowed to her in what Arletta knew was a very French fashion and Pauline dropped her a little curtsey.

Then the two children went from the room and she turned to the housemaid,

"Will you show me where I can wash? And I would like, if possible, to have a bath."

"A bath, *m'mselle?*" the housemaid exclaimed. 'That's very English! But if you want one, I'll order it to be brought upstairs."

Arletta did not protest as she had a feeling that any ordinary Governess might have done.

Laboriously first a hip bath was brought to her bedroom and then a manservant carried up several cans of hot water which were brought into the room by the maid.

There was, she discovered, behind a curtain at one side of her room a basin but no bath.

She thought that the Duc would be extremely annoyed if he knew how often she was going to ask for a bath to be brought upstairs unless he expressly forbade it.

But she could not believe that in such a huge Château he could really be aware of everything that happened.

And yet quite obviously from the way the children spoke he overshadowed their lives and, she was quite certain, everybody else's, including Monsieur Byien's.

It was all rather fascinating and while she soaked away what she thought of as 'travel stains' in the hip bath, she found herself vastly intrigued by everything that she had seen so far.

But she was well aware that she was going to have a difficult time erasing from the children's minds everything that the Duc had deliberately implanted in their thoughts against their father's country.

Dinner turned out to be a formal meal that for a Governess and two small children she found incredible.

Waited on by a butler and three footmen, they sat in the huge Baronial dining room, which could have accommodated nearly a hundred people.

The Duc's chair at the far end of the table, which, carved and painted with the Arms of the Sauterre family, looked like a Royal Throne.

They sat in what were their proper places at the far end of the table and as course followed course of delicious food, Arletta who was hungry enjoyed every mouthful, although she was aware that by the end of the meal that Pauline was half-asleep.

David, however, ate heartily and chatted away, answering her questions about the Château.

He had obviously, she thought, been indoctrinated with the great consequence of the Sauterre family to the exclusion of a great deal of French history that might have been more useful to him.

As for the English, they were obviously the enemy.

"Uncle Etienne's ancestors were at the Field of the Cloth of Gold," David announced. "And they fought to try to save St. Joan of Arc, who was burnt to death by the English, although she was a Saint!"

"All that happened a long time ago," Arletta pointed out firmly.

"The English may well have won the Battle of Waterloo," David persisted, "but Uncle Etienne claims that they were very cruel to Napoleon Bonaparte when he was a prisoner on the Isle of St. Helena."

"I think what you have to do," Arletta said eventually, "is to learn a little about the English before you come to England. Don't forget, David, that you belong to an ancient and very distinguished family. In fact the Redruths were Chieftains or perhaps Kings in Cornwall long before William the Conqueror invaded us from Normandy."

Jane had given her this information, but she had not realised at the time how important it was going to be.

"He was French and he won!" David asserted.

"But now the English Empire spreads over half the world," Arletta said, "and I think you must learn about it as well."

She sighed before she added,

"Actually you are very, very lucky."

"Why?" David asked in a somewhat hostile tone.

"Because you are both English and French and you therefore must try to understand both countries and do your best to keep them at peace with each other."

David looked surprised and Arletta went on,

"Some of the Redruths have been Statesmen and Diplomats. I must learn about them and how they managed to prevent war and create friendship between nations who previously had always loathed each other."

She was not sure that this was true, but David would not be able to contradict her!

"Do you think that war is wrong, *mademoiselle?*" he asked.

"I think it is horrible, wicked and cruel and many men lose in war the most precious thing any of us can possess, which is life."

David thought this over for a moment and then he commented,

"Suppose they don't mind dying?"

"Everybody minds dying, especially when they are young," Arletta answered. "Life is exciting and an adventure. There is so much to do, so much to learn and so much to enjoy."

She saw that David was listening and then asked,

"Why should one lose something so precious just because of some political quarrel or because the Ruler of one country is greedy and wants to take away what another Ruler owns?"

She thought as she spoke that this was a theme that she must enlarge upon and perhaps describe the concept better than she was doing at the moment.

It was obvious that David was impressed and after a moment he said,

"Uncle Etienne wants me to go into the French Army!"

Without thinking Arletta replied,

"But, of course, you cannot do that! I know that your father would be horrified if he found that you were fighting against your own kith and kin in another country!"

She spoke so violently that David stared at her.

Then she felt that maybe she had been overemotional about something that was so much a part of her own upbringing that she could hardly believe she was listening to an English boy saying what David had just said to her.

She cried quickly,

"I think if you have finished, we should go upstairs. I am sure that Pauline wants to go to bed."

"I'm tired," Pauline moaned.

"Yes, of course, you are," Arletta said. "Who puts you to bed? Shall I do it?"

"No, *ma Bonne*," Pauline said. "I want her! I want *ma Bonne*!"

Waiting outside the Dining Room door was a middle-aged gentle-faced Frenchwoman, who swept Pauline up into her arms.

"*La petite* gets ever so tired, *m'mselle*," she explained to Arletta. "She is not strong and should have plenty of sleep, but Monsieur insists that the children dine downstairs and with you arrivin' she did not have a rest before dinner."

"Then that is something we must prevent another time," Arletta smiled.

"I'm tired – I'm very tired," Pauline whimpered.

The Frenchwoman carried her away and Arletta asked,

"Are you ready to go to bed too, David?"

"Not yet," he replied.

"Then perhaps you will show me a little of the Château or is it too late?"

David grinned.

"No one can stop us now that Uncle Etienne is away and I would very much like to show it to you."

"Very well," Arletta nodded. "Let's see as much as we can before it grows too dark."

She realised that it was just impossible to see everything.

The Château seemed to extend for miles and there were three other towers similar to the one that the children used, as well as enormous Reception rooms in the centre block, which looked out, she discovered, over the most entrancing formal gardens.

There were pools ornamented with ancient urns and a huge fountain sculpted with cupids and dolphins, which flung water like a thousand iridescent rainbows high into the sky.

It was so lovely and at the same time traditional and formal and very unlike the gardens at Weir House that Arletta was so familiar with.

Everything seemed to have its place and she thought it impossible even for one revolutionary weed to raise up its head between the paved walks or the tightly clipped yew hedges.

She was not surprised to find that everything in the Château was very luxurious.

As she had seen when she arrived, the furnishing was predominately Louis XIV and she wondered how so much had escaped the French Revolution until David explained,

"Uncle Etienne says that in the Revolution most of the great treasures were hidden in safe places like caverns in the mountains or deep dungeons that no one could find an entrance to."

In fact the Château had not been ransacked in the same way as those nearer to Paris.

"As it is so isolated here," David went on, "there were not many people to revolt against the reigning Duc of the time."

"He was very lucky," Arletta pointed out.

David shrugged his shoulders.

"It has made Uncle Etienne more puffed up with pride than he would be otherwise. I heard one of the servants say once that he thinks he is God!"

Arletta gave a little exclamation.

"I am sure, David, that you should not say such things about your uncle."

"Why not to you?" David asked. "You are the enemy, who has been forced upon him and he already hates you before he has even met you!"

Arletta was startled.

"Do you really mean that?"

"He said to us when Aunt Margaret had left, 'your aunt has forced an English Governess upon me against my will, who will teach you the barbaric language which you, David, have to assimilate before you suffer Hell in what the English call a Public School'!"

"That is not true!" Arletta exclaimed. "I am sure that your father loved being at Eton and all my family who have been there are very proud and very fond of their old school. They would be shocked and horrified to think that you thought of it like that."

"I am prepared to go to Hell, or anywhere else, as long as it is a long way from here," David replied.

They were in the library and, looking at the thousands of books in the enormous room, Arletta thought it strange that any child should not be intrigued by living in such a fine Château with so much to occupy and entertain him or her.

She sat down on a stool in front of the empty fireplace and then quizzed him,

"Tell me, David, why do you hate living here?"

For a moment he looked over his shoulder in the same surreptitious way that he had done before to make certain that there was nobody near them.

Then he came closer to her and he almost whispered,

"It's horrible. I could just bear it when Mama was alive, but now it is worse than any prison could possibly be!"

"But why? Why do you say that?" Arletta asked.

David hesitated and she wondered if he would tell her the truth.

Then he said,

"It's Uncle Etienne! He hates us because Papa was English and the whole Château is just horrible!"

He lowered his voice before he went on,

"And Uncle Etienne is a murderer! He has killed two women!"

CHAPTER THREE

Arletta, standing at the window of her bedroom, thought that on the whole it had been an extraordinary but very good day.

First she had been delighted to find that David was not so ignorant where English was concerned as she had been led to believe.

His father had died when he was six, but until then he had talked to him in English and only after that, when his mother had brought the children to the Château, had that language been barred.

But once he began to talk with Arletta the words came back even if his grammar was rather hazy and, as he was very eager to learn, she thought that in one day they had made a surprising amount of progress.

She insisted on teaching David alone and then tried very gently to interest Pauline in the English names for flowers, food and everything around her.

The little girl tried hard, but it was obviously very much more difficult for her and Arletta thought that it was more important to get David ready for his English school.

There were so many small things too that had to be corrected, for instance the way that he wrote out his sums in arithmetic and the way that he addressed people, which was entirely French and would she reckoned be laughed at in England.

It was all going to take time, but she found that she was not only extremely interested in what she was doing but she had to admit very curious as well.

When David had told her last night that his uncle had murdered two women, she had thought at first that it was some kind of joke and later that the boy was lying for the sake of shocking her.

Finally she recognised that this was a puzzle that she had to unravel, but it could not be done in a few minutes.

She therefore talked about other subjects until they both went up to bed.

*

In the morning what he had said to her was still vividly in her mind and she found herself wondering how any child could hold such an idea about his uncle.

She could understand that he found it hard in the circumstances, if that was what he believed, to live happily in the Château.

After she had finished her lesson with David, they went outside and continued talking in English as he showed her first the formal gardens and then took her to the stables.

She had expected that the Duc's horses would be exceptional, as she had admired the fine team that had met her at the Station.

But she was not prepared for row upon row of stables filled with Arab-bred superfine horses that were better than any she had seen in the whole of her life.

"Uncle Etienne has his racing stables at Chantilly," David informed her, "but these he rides himself and, of course, we are allowed to ride them too."

Arletta's eyes lit up instantly and then she asked,

"Do you suppose I might ride with you?"

"Of course, if you want to," David replied, "but I did not imagine at all that an English Governess would be keen on riding."

Then he laughed and continued,

"But then you are not the sort of English Governess I was expecting."

"What did the Duc say?" Arletta asked him.

"He said you would be prim, ugly and very strict!"

Arletta was not certain if he was being truthful or merely teasing her.

They arranged to ride after luncheon, but Pauline said that she would rather stay with her *Bonne* and therefore David and Arletta rode alone.

He took her over the beautiful countryside and into one of the thick dark woods that she thought of as dragon forests.

She was not surprised to find that the trees were planted to facilitate not only riding but also shooting and they were carefully looked after by woodcutters who were working in one of the woods they visited.

By the time they returned she was certain that the Duc ran his estates diligently and efficiently.

But one little episode had upset her.

They had stopped to speak to the men who were working in a small vine field and the overseer who obviously knew David came up to speak to them.

"Nice to see you here, *monsieur*," he said politely and looked at Arletta with curiosity.

"This is Pierre Beauvais, *mademoiselle*," David told her. "He looks after all Uncle Etienne's vines and makes the most delicious wine."

Arletta held out her hand.

"I have come to the Château," she said in French, "to teach English to *le petit monsieur et mademoiselle* Pauline."

Pierre Beauvais looked at her in astonishment.

"You are a Governess, *m'mselle?*"

Arletta nodded.

Then, as David moved away to speak to one of the other men working on the vines, he said in a low voice,

"*C'est impossible!* You should go home, *m'mselle*, you will not be happy here."

"Why do you say that?" Arletta asked him.

Pierre Beauvais glanced round and she felt that he was embarrassed that he had said too much.

Then, as David came back to join them, he said quickly,

"Go home, *m'mselle*, it will be better for you."

There was no chance to say anything more and, riding back to the Château, Arletta thought that it was a very odd conversation to have had with one of the Duc's employees.

Pauline was waiting for them and they went not into the schoolroom but into the library.

Arletta was determined to find picture books for the little girl, which would make it more interesting for her to learn English when she saw the words nicely illustrated.

There were, however, so many thousands of books covering the walls that it was difficult to know where to begin to look and there seemed to be no catalogue.

Then, as the children were helping her search, the door opened and a man came into the library and she looked at him in surprise.

He was young, good-looking and extremely elegantly dressed.

She was wondering who he could be when David piped up in a rather offhand manner,

"Oh, hello, Cousin Jacques. I did not know that you were coming back today."

"I am back," the newcomer said, "and I understand we have a visitor."

Arletta walked towards him.

"I am Jane Turner, *monsieur*," she began, wondering as she spoke how he fitted into the organisation of the Château.

"You are the new Governess?"

There was no doubt at the astonishment in his voice and on his face and Arletta thought of what a fuss people made about her appearance.

"I gather," she replied a little coldly, "that you were not expecting to find me here."

"I was expecting to find an English Governess, but not somebody who looks like you!"

"I find it difficult, *monsieur*," Arletta said, "to understand what my looks have to do with it. The only reason I am here is to teach the children."

"Perhaps I should introduce myself," the young man said. "I am Jacques de Sauterre – Comte Jacques if you wish to be formal. I am a cousin of the Duc and, when I am not in Paris, I live here in the Château."

Arletta smiled.

"I arrived only yesterday, so you will understand, *monsieur le Comte*, that I am finding it difficult to understand the complexities of the household."

"That is not surprising," the Comte replied, "and I suppose the children have not enlightened you. They are tiresome little monsters unless you bully them!"

He seemed to speak jokingly, but to Arletta's surprise David scowled at him and Pauline, who had only glanced up when he came into the room, now had her back to him as she looked through the book that she had just taken down from one of the shelves.

"As you see, we are one big happy family," the Comte said sarcastically and then added, "I suppose, as you have only just arrived, that you have not yet seen the Duchesse."

"The Duchesse?" Arletta gasped.

It had never occurred to her that there might be a woman living in the Château.

"The Duc's grandmother," the Comte explained. "She is very old and in bad health and she seldom bothers with visitors unless, of course, she is curious about them."

He looked at Arletta in a manner that was slightly insulting and then resumed,

"But I feel very sure, Miss Turner, that she will be very very curious about you!"

There was something in the way he spoke that made Arletta stiffen and she replied,

"You must excuse me, *monsieur*, but I am busy trying to find a book that will interest Pauline."

"If you are expecting to find any books in English here, you are much mistaken," the Comte sneered.

"I was not expecting anything of the sort," Arletta answered, "but I cannot find a catalogue and it is therefore difficult to know what is available."

"There must be a catalogue somewhere," the Comte remarked. "I cannot believe that my most efficient and most estimable cousin would not have everything that concerns him in perfect order."

There was a sarcastic and rather nasty note in his voice and Arletta merely walked towards Pauline and looked down at the book that the child held in her hand.

"Shall we take this one upstairs with us?" she asked.

"No, it's very dull," Pauline pouted. "I want a book with lots of birds and flowers in it or else pictures of England."

The Comte laughed.

"That is something you will certainly not find here and, if your uncle hears you asking for such a thing, he will be very angry!"

Pauline ignored him and looked up at Arletta to say,

"Please find me one, *mademoiselle*."

"I will do my best," Arletta answered, "but it is rather difficult to know where to begin."

She tried to ignore the Comte, who was standing near her and looking at her in a way that she considered impertinent.

Then, as if he had just made up his mind, he said,

"I would like to have a word with you, *mademoiselle*. Will you come to the other end of the room?"

Arletta hesitated.

She wanted to say that she had nothing to talk to him about and then she thought that it would be rude and it would be a mistake not to be polite to one of the Duc's relations.

Reluctantly, telling David to go on looking for what they required and speaking to him in English, she walked to the end of the library, where by the huge carved fireplace there was a sofa and several chairs.

She sat down on the sofa and then thought that she had made a mistake as the Comte sat beside her a little closer than she considered necessary.

Lowering his voice, he then spoke to her,

"You have made a great mistake in coming here!"

"A mistake?" Arletta asked.

"You will find it very boring and there are many other places in France which will amuse you and where with your very pretty face you would be a great success."

"I don't know what you are talking about, *monsieur,*" Arletta said. "I came here to teach English to the children, who are the nephew and niece of my friend, Lady Langley, and that is what I intend to do."

"Then, if you insist, you must let me help you. It will not be easy for you to cope with the Duc and, as he has already made up his mind to hate you, you will find the Château very uncomfortable when he returns."

"I am sure that you mean to be kind, *monsieur,*" Arletta replied, "but I am quite prepared to cross my bridges when I come to them. Since the Duc is not yet here, I shall do my best until he does return."

"Your best is certainly good enough for me," the Comte conceded. "As I have already told you, I will look after you, help and guide you."

Arletta rose to her feet.

"Thank you for being so kind, but to be quite honest, being English, I am quite capable of looking after myself."

She walked away from him and he did not attempt to stop her.

She heard him laugh softly and thought that he was undoubtedly the sort of Frenchman that Jane had warned her about.

At the same time she did not like him and she thought that he might make things difficult instead, as he had offered, of helping her.

To her relief, when she reached the other end of the library where the children were, she found that he had left them and, as soon as she had found several books that she thought might be useful, they went upstairs to the schoolroom.

As soon as they were back, David volunteered,

"I don't like Cousin Jacques."

"Nor do I," Pauline chimed in, not wishing to be left out.

"Why?" Arletta asked.

She noticed that David once again looked over his shoulder as if he was afraid of being overheard.

Then he tried to explain his feelings,

"There is something about him that makes me feel uncomfortable. I don't know why."

He looked a little puzzled and then he went on,

"Mama said that we should send out waves of kindness to people so that they like us, but the waves coming from Cousin Jacques are not kind."

That was what Arletta had thought herself, but she was surprised that such a small boy should be so perceptive.

Then she thought that living in the Château in such strange conditions had perhaps made him different from other boys.

She was afraid that if this was so he might find school in England even more difficult.

"I suppose if we all behaved properly we would try to like everybody," she said lightly. "Although it is not always possible, at least we can make the best of them."

David was not listening. Instead he was playing with his soldiers, which were on the table where he had arranged them the previous night.

"They are a very fine collection," Arletta commented. "Who gave them to you, David?"

"Cousin Etienne. He had them made for me and I think his idea, when he did so, was not to please me but to make me interested in becoming a soldier myself in the French Army."

Again Arletta was aware that it was an unusual thought for a boy of eleven.

She wondered whether it was something that she should try to encourage or suppress.

What would Jane have done about it in her place? She knew that Jane was very down to earth. As her father would have said, she 'has her feet planted firmly on the ground' and, except where Simon Sutton was concerned, her head was full of facts not fantasies.

Arletta was sure that she would have faced even the Château itself in a practical and straightforward manner.

She knew by the end of the day that for her the Château held a secret magic that was inescapable apart from being in so many ways menacing and oppressive.

She had found out that part of the main building was of a later date than the towers. Here the windows were high and the rooms with their many tapestries, pictures and huge crystal chandeliers were so beautiful that she felt it impossible not to feel when she entered them that she walked into a Fairytale.

To the children it was all so familiar that they were not interested and preferred to take her to the Armoury, where ancient weapons that had been used by the Sauterres over the generations were arranged on the walls.

In the middle of the room there was a cannon with its round iron balls piled beside it.

They also wanted to show her the dungeons, but even David realised that it had grown too dark and it would be better if they went earlier the next day.

Just before dinner, when the children had gone to their own rooms to change and Arletta was just going up the stone steps to her bedroom, a footman came to the door with a message,

"Madame la Duchesse wishes to see you, *m'mselle*!"

Following him Arletta felt intrigued at the idea of meeting the Duc's grandmother.

She wondered if in any way she would be like her own grandmother whom she could vaguely remember coming to stay with them many years ago before her father came into the title and they had moved into the family mansion.

She had thought that her grandmother was exquisite with her white hair, her delicate features and her long thin hands.

She had been very dignified and sat as if her back was supported by a ramrod. But her eyes had often twinkled with amusement and her laughter was soft and melodious.

"I wish she had not died when I was so young," Arletta had often said later.

She thought now that Madame la Duchesse might be something like her *Grandmère* after whom she was named.

The footman led her a long way, in fact to the other end of the Château, which Arletta had not yet been able to explore.

Then they went up a rather fine staircase to the first floor, where there was an elderly maid waiting for them.

"Good evening, *m'mselle*," she said politely and then turned to the footman, "You must wait, Jean, to take *m'mselle* back. She'll never find her own way."

"No, that is true," Arletta said. "Please wait or I shall be completely lost."

She then followed the maid through a beautifully painted door into a small hall out of which opened two other doors.

In the next moment she found herself in the Duchesse's bedroom.

It was different from any room that she had seen before with a huge bed on a dais and curtains falling behind it from a corolla fixed to the ceiling.

Propped up against a number of pillows was the strangest old lady that Arletta had ever seen.

She was very old and her face, which might once have been beautiful, was wrinkled and lined just like Chinese parchment. Her hair was white but so skilfully arranged that Arletta suspected it to be a wig.

Round her neck she wore a dozen ropes of huge pearls and glittering in her ears were diamond earrings that swung and sparkled with every movement she made.

Her hands, which were blue-veined, were weighed down with rings and there were a half dozen bracelets on each of her wrists.

Despite the fact that it was summer, her bed was covered with an ermine bedspread, which was growing slightly yellow in colour.

As Arletta moved nearer to the bed, she was aware that despite the fact that she was very old, the Duchesse's eyes had a shrewd look in them as if she took in every detail of her appearance.

Arletta curtseyed and waited until the Duchesse quizzed her,

"You are Jane Turner, who has come here to teach my great-grandchildren?"

"Yes, *madame*, I am."

"I don't believe it. You have come to the Château to see my grandson, that is your reason for being here."

"I assure you, *madame*," Arletta replied, "that I am here because Lady Langley asked me to teach English to her niece and nephew, having been surprised when she stayed here recently to find that they neither of them could speak their own language."

"Their own language?" the Duchesse retorted. "You had better not let my grandson hear you say that! He hates the English and who shall blame him? If you are hoping to 'catch' him, I can tell you you are going the wrong way about it."

"You are quite mistaken, *madame,* if that is what you think about me," Arletta protested. "I cannot imagine who has been telling you such stupid tales, which are quite untrue."

She thought as she spoke that, if Jane had been confronted with such a ridiculous assertion, she would have been upset and embarrassed.

Then she remembered that poor plain Jane would never have been suspected of trying to 'catch' anyone, least of all the Duc de Sauterre.

The Duchesse looked her up and down and then commented,

"You are very pretty, I admit that, but this is not the right place to flaunt your looks. The sooner you go back to where you came from the better for you and everybody else. I assure you that my grandson has no time for Governesses."

"And I assure you, *madame*," Arletta said slowly and clearly, "I am not interested in your grandson, whom I have not yet met, but only with the children whom I have come to teach."

She curtseyed, turned away from the bed and walked towards the door.

As she reached it, the Duchesse screamed,

"*Attendez*! How dare you walk away before I have finished talking to you? Come back here immediately!"

Arletta turned round, but she made no effort to return to where she had been standing. Instead she just looked at the Duchesse, holding her head high.

Unexpectedly the old woman chuckled.

"At least, whoever you are, you have spirit! Most people are frightened of me."

Arletta did not speak and after a moment the old woman went on.

"Come here. I want to look at you."

Slowly, as if she was reluctant to do so, Arletta walked back to stand again beside the bed.

"You are very pretty and you are a lady," the Duchesse said in a low voice, as if she was speaking to herself. "I wonder why Jacques is so eager to be rid of you?"

Arletta wondered too, but there was little point in saying so.

There was silence and then after a moment Arletta said,

"Excuse me, *madame*, but, if I don't go now, I shall be late for dinner and I am sure that is a crime in this very punctual well organised household."

The Duchesse smiled.

"You are right about that. But I want to see you again — do you understand? I will send for you tomorrow and you can tell me all about yourself."

"Thank you, *madame*, good night."

Arletta curtseyed again and walked towards the door, this time not looking back.

The footman, Jean, was waiting for her outside in the passage and he led her back by a complicated route to the foot of the staircase of the tower.

When they reached it, Arletta said,

"Thank you," and the man remarked,

"Strange old lady, isn't she? People think she's a witch! But there's a real one in the village and if you wants your fortune told, there be no one better."

Arletta realised that he was not being impertinent, only friendly, and so she answered,

"I think it would be disappointing to know the future before it happens. What makes you think that the woman in the village is a witch?"

"She's one all right!" the footman answered. "You'll have to be careful not to offend her."

"I will not do so," Arletta replied, "and thank you once again."

She ran up the twisting stone staircase, thinking that everything in the Château grew stranger and stranger.

She had never met anybody quite so fantastic as the Duc's grandmother.

But everybody seemed to be warning her against staying and it made her all the more determined to find out what was wrong and why they wished to be rid of her.

She had also not forgotten that David had told her that his uncle was a *murderer*.

"How can it be possible?" she asked aloud and changed into her gown, regretting that she had forgotten to tell the maid to bring her a bath.

'I must make her understand that I want one every evening,' she told herself.

There were enough servants for it not to be a very arduous duty with so few residents at the Château.

At the same time there were now two more than she had seen last night and she wondered how many more lived here.

The Comte had dinner with them and monopolised Arletta so that David and Pauline hardly spoke a word.

It was something she thought should not happen, but she found it difficult to know how she could prevent the Comte from talking to her and paying her compliments that she found embarrassing and unnerving.

Also she had the feeling that they were not in any way sincere.

When dinner was over, she insisted, when he tried to inveigle her into going with him into one of the State rooms, that she must take the children upstairs to the schoolroom.

Pauline's *Bonne* was waiting for her to put her to bed and Arletta was then alone with David.

"I can see you don't like Cousin Jacques," he remarked when the door had closed behind them.

"I have not said so," Arletta retorted.

"I told you there was something about him that is not nice," David continued.

"You know quite well I must not criticise anybody here," Arletta scolded him.

"I will not repeat to anybody what you say to me," David assured her, "but you have to be careful in case somebody is listening."

"Who would want to do that?"

David shrugged his shoulders.

"The maids listen and tell Great-grandmama and the men spy for Uncle Etienne."

"I don't believe it!" Arletta exclaimed. "What is there to spy about?"

Again David shrugged his shoulders.

"I think you are all too isolated here," Arletta carried on. "I am sure that you and Pauline should have friends of your own age. There must be some children who live in the vicinity."

"If there are, Uncle Etienne will not let us near them. But Cousin Jacques has friends."

Arletta wanted to ask who they were, but then thought that it would be a mistake.

When she climbed into bed, she recalled in her mind everything that had been said and had happened and thought that it was all so extraordinary that she really ought to write it down for Jane and send it to her out in Jamaica.

'If I was clever, I could write a novel about it,' she mused, 'although at the moment, if I am the heroine, there is certainly the lack of a hero!'

*

The following day it was a relief to learn when the Comte did not appear that he had gone away to stay with friends.

"It will be much nicer without him," David said darkly. "He says one thing, but his eyes say another."

"You are too fanciful," Arletta argued, although she knew that he was right. "Boys of your age should be thinking of cricket, riding, shooting and, of course, lessons."

"I think of all those things," David replied, "except for cricket, which Uncle Etienne says is a very English game. But I am going to play it when I go to Eton, because Papa was in the First Eleven."

"My father was too," Arletta said, "and, although I am only a woman, I can show you how the game is played and perhaps we can ask one of the servants to bowl for us."

David thought that this was an excellent idea and Arletta went to find Monsieur Byien.

She thought it rather strange that, while she, as a Governess, was allowed to have meals in the dining room, Monsieur Byien apparently ate alone.

She found him in his office and when she explained what she wanted, he looked more worried than ever.

"I think you will have to wait and ask the Duc about this," he cautioned.

"He might not come back for ages," Arletta replied. "I think it is important that David should have some idea of how the game is played and, as he is so enthusiastic, it's a mistake for him to be put off with promises."

Monsieur Byien laughed.

"Very well, *mademoiselle*, you win. And, as I played cricket as a boy, I will try first to see how rusty I am when it comes to bowling."

The gardeners made some stumps and to Arletta's surprise Monsieur Byien produced a cricket bat and a ball that were rather ancient but still serviceable.

After a little practice David began to handle his bat quite proficiently and hit the ball more times than he missed it.

It was Monsieur Byien who gave up first, complaining that he was growing too old for such strenuous exercise. But he promised to make enquiries of the younger men in the villages who could practise with David the next day.

"I would rather have you," David said. "I think you are jolly sporting!"

He said this in English and Arletta laughed.

"I don't think that you could have a greater compliment, Monsieur Byien," she told him and he had to admit that it was true.

When they went back to the Château Arletta felt that she had achieved a great deal in a very short space of time, but there was undoubtedly much more to do.

It was a relief that evening when, after the heat of the day, Pauline was so tired that she had supper in the schoolroom with her *Bonne* and Arletta and David had dinner alone in the dining room.

They talked in English with only occasional breaks when David wanted to say something quickly and found his English too inadequate to keep up with his mind.

Arletta knew that she had the small boy's friendship and that he liked being with her.

She thought that today at any rate he had forgotten to glance surreptitiously over his shoulder and say things about his uncle that horrified her.

There was no summons from the Duchesse and, when David went to bed, she thought with a feeling of satisfaction that she could rest her mind for an hour or two before she went to sleep.

She undressed and saw that one of the pretty nightgowns that had belonged to her mother had been laid out for her on the bed and she put it on.

Then she realised that she had nothing to read.

She had meant to collect a book from the library for herself, but had forgotten to do so.

It was disappointing, she thought, and then she remembered that at this time of night she undoubtedly had the Château to herself.

Instead of going to her room she walked back towards the main building where the State rooms were situated.

She knew that all the servants, except for the footmen on duty in the hall, would have moved into a part of the Château that had been built very much later where both their bedrooms and the kitchens were.

"They like it there," David explained, "because there are no ghosts in that part of the Château."

"I have not yet seen any here," Arletta smiled.

"I have always thought," David replied, "that ghosts appear only to people they dislike and want to frighten."

"Then, if they are leaving me alone, it is a compliment I really do appreciate," Arletta laughed.

Now she put on the beautiful blue negligée that had also belonged to her mother and, opening her door quietly, she slipped down the twisting stairs.

Her soft slippers made no sound and anyway there was no one to hear her.

Now, as she walked through the long passages towards the State rooms, she thought it understandable that anybody, children or grown-ups, living here with no other distractions would use their imaginations.

They would people the place with ghosts from the past or turn the shadows that came from the thick fortifications of the walls into something menacing.

The sun had sunk over the horizon, but the sky was crimson and gold as Arletta entered the room that she thought was the most beautiful of all the State rooms.

It was in the centre of the building and was known, she had been told, as the ballroom, except for the very centre of the floor, it was furnished with exquisite Louis XIV sofas and chairs and *Aubusson* carpets that were filled with bright colour.

On the walls were very old tapestries, mostly in pink, and long gilt-framed mirrors between the windows reflected them and they seemed to blend with the colours in the sky.

It was so lovely that Arletta felt as if she was a Princess visiting the Château two centuries earlier and being entertained royally by the Duc of the day.

There was a white piano in one corner of the room inset with plaques of *Sèvres* china and, feeling that the scene she was visualising needed music, she sat down to play a Strauss waltz.

It seemed to blend with the room and the light from the windows and gradually, as she played, the last rays of the sun disappeared and there was just the mystic dusk.

It was then that she suddenly had an idea.

She had noticed that in the corner of the ballroom, as she had entered, was a long pole with a taper on the end of it, which was used to light the candles in the chandeliers hanging from the ceiling.

Then there was, in a holder below the taper, a little brass hood to extinguish them with.

This was a scenario that Arletta had seen used at home when they lit the chandeliers in the large drawing room when her mother had entertained.

On the piano was a small candelabrum and beside it a matchbox and there was no reason, she thought, why anybody should know about it, if she enjoyed herself as she wished to do.

She lit the candles in the candelabrum, then lit the taper on the pole and lifted it up to carry it to the chandelier in the middle of the room.

She could reach only the candles on the lowest tier, but she managed to light nearly a dozen of them and the whole room seemed to miraculously come to life.

She could imagine the ladies magnificent in their high wigs and wearing huge gowns with panniers on either side.

Then there were the men with their wigs or powdered hair caught back in a bow at the nape of the neck and the sleeves of their elaborately embroidered coats ending with fine lace falling over their hands.

She sat down again at the piano to play music that conjured up a vision of those she could see in her mind's eye dancing a minuet in the centre of the room.

Then inevitably she came back to herself and now in the next century she was dressed in the full skirts of a crinoline and the music was once again the exquisite melodies of Strauss.

Her fingers flew over the keyboard until she could not stop her fantasy and she rose and, stepping onto the polished floor, began to dance.

Her negligée was too narrow and she pulled it off and threw it on a chair.

Now she was attired only in her nightgown of transparently thin lawn inset with row upon row of lace and frothing out with a wide hem of the same.

There were little puff sleeves of lace and her neckline was cut low and also edged with lace.

She knew, however, without being told that with her fair hair and blue eyes she looked like the Princess out of a picture book.

Now she was part of her own imagination and she swung round humming the music that she had been playing beneath her breath.

She felt as if she was partnered by the tall dark handsome man who had always been in her dreams.

Suddenly, as she swung with her arms outstretched gracefully beneath the chandelier, she opened her eyes and saw him standing just inside the door of the ballroom.

But instead of looking at her with admiration or perhaps love, there was a look of incredulity and anger on his face.

Her feet came to a standstill and Arletta stiffened as she stared at the man who was real and not a figment of her imagination.

Then, as she looked at him, there was no need for anybody to tell her that this was the Duc!

CHAPTER FOUR

Arletta felt as if she was frozen into immobility.

At the same time she was embarrassingly aware that her hair was falling over her shoulders, that she was wearing nothing but a nightgown and that for the first time she was facing her employer in a very humiliating position.

He was still looking at her as if he could not believe what he saw and she realised that he was quite different from what she had expected.

Because everybody had said such extraordinary things about him, she had imagined him to be dark and sinister, perhaps round-shouldered like the wicked Duke of Gloucester who had murdered the two little Princes in the Tower of London.

Instead the Duc was taller than the average Frenchman and, although his hair was dark, he had a fresh complexion. His features were clear-cut and he was, in fact, very handsome.

What, however, made him frightening, Arletta thought, was the expression in his eyes and his eyelids seemed to droop a little over them.

There were deep cynical lines from his nose to the corners of his mouth, which was set at the moment in a sharp line.

Then in a voice that seemed to vibrate on the air, he asked,

"Who are you? What is your name?"

"Arletta – Jane Turner!"

There was a perceivable pause between the first two words because, bemused by the Duc's sudden appearance, Arletta had for the moment forgotten the part that she was playing and her own name came automatically to her lips.

As she spoke, she made a great effort and forced herself to pick up her negligée from the chair and put it on.

"Are you saying that you are the English Governess who has been sent here by Lady Langley?" the Duc asked.

"Yes – that is right," Arletta agreed, "and – I apologise – but no one was – expecting you to – return tonight."

The words came in frightened gasps.

The Duc was still staring at her from under his drooping eyelids in a way that she found uncomfortably intimidating, but now that she was more decently dressed and she could get her breath back, her voice sounded a little more normal as she repeated,

"I can only – apologise, *monsieur le Duc.* I was – carried away by the – beauty of the house into and – stepping back into the – past."

"And you lit the candles on the chandeliers as well as removing some of your clothing to create the illusion?"

The way the Duc spoke made it sound as if she had committed an act of indecency if not a crime.

Arletta blushed before she faltered,

"There is – nothing I can do but – apologise, and I hope, *monsieur*, you will accept my – assurance that such a – thing will not – happen again."

There was silence before the Duc said,

"You are really the English Governess I was expecting?"

"Y-yes."

Somehow it was difficult to lie and Arletta thought even to herself that her voice sounded unsure and unsteady.

With another effort she walked across the dance floor and moving to the piano closed the lid.

As she did so, she was vividly conscious that the Duc was watching her and once again she was aware how incompetent she must look.

'How could I have been so foolish?' she asked herself desperately.

Suddenly she was surprised to find that the Duc had moved and was much nearer to her than he had been a moment ago and she asked him,

"Shall I – extinguish the – candles?"

"A servant can do that. I think tomorrow, Miss Turner, when you are dressed more suitably for the part you are employed for, I should have a talk with you."

"Of course – *monsieur.*"

She dropped him a small curtsey and, without looking at him again, walked out of the ballroom into the passage.

She moved slowly and with what she hoped was some dignity until, as if she could bear it no longer, she suddenly started to run and speeding along the passages reached the staircase that led to the tower.

Only when she was in her own room did she feel as if she had encountered one of the dragons that she had always imagined lived in the forest and was not certain whether she had been annihilated by it or was actually unscathed.

'How could I have known, how could I have guessed,' she asked herself, 'that the Duc would return to the Château in such an unexpected way?'

It was a long time before she could fall sleep.

When she awoke, it was with a feeling of heaviness and apprehension in her heart in case the Duc would decide that she was unsuitable and sent her back to England immediately.

There was no doubt that she had astonished him and she supposed that, if he had disliked the idea of having an Englishwoman in the house in the first place, his prejudice would certainly have been intensified by the scene that he had found in the ballroom.

Therefore there was every likelihood of her being told to leave.

As she dressed, she found herself praying that this would not happen.

She wanted to stay and she knew if she was sent away now that the Château would always haunt her.

It would be infuriating never to know the reasons for so much that puzzled her and that she could find no sensible explanation for.

The first thing, however, unless she was to be dismissed ignominiously without even the opportunity of giving an explanation, was to make herself look the respectable English Governess that the Duc was obviously expecting.

She pulled back her hair and used a dozen hairpins to hold it tightly in place, wishing as she did so that she had not allowed it to fall free last night.

What would any man think of a woman who danced in such an abandoned manner and in her nightgown?

Such behaviour on the part of a Governess was most certainly indefensible.

'How could I have done anything so immodest?' she asked her reflection in the mirror over and over again.

She tried to tell herself defiantly that it was the Duc's fault for surreptitiously entering his own Château without notifying anybody of his imminent arrival.

She was quite sure that it was an unexpected visit because the servants had not talked about him and this was confirmed when the children came from their rooms dressed and ready for breakfast to say,

"Have you heard, *mademoiselle*, that Uncle Etienne has come home?"

"When did he arrive?" Arletta asked evasively.

"He came back after we had gone to bed," David replied.

"Now that Uncle Etienne is back he will spoil everything," Pauline answered Arletta. "He will be cross and, when he is angry, he gives me pains in my tummy."

As she put her small hand to her body, Arletta knew exactly what the child meant and thought that what she had just said might well describe what she herself was feeling at this moment.

Now, wearing her most businesslike and what she thought an unattractive gown and her hair pinned back severely, she took the children down to the breakfast room only to find that the Duc was not there.

"Where is Uncle Etienne?" David asked one of the footmen waiting on them.

"Monsieur le Duc has already had his breakfast," he replied.

"Good!" David remarked irrepressibly.

He sat down and began to eat heartily the hot *croissants* on which he spread a generous helping of the yellow butter that came from the Duc's own herd of cows and honey that came from the hives that Arletta had seen not only in the garden but almost everywhere on the estate.

She felt actually that it would be better for the children to start the day with eggs or some other sensible dish rather than with so much bread however delicious it might be.

But she knew that to suggest such a thing would be to be told that English customs were not tolerated in the Château and the Duc would never entertain them.

She herself found that she was feeling too apprehensive to be hungry.

Then, just as the children had finished breakfast and she was going to the schoolroom to start David on his English lessons, there came the summons from a footman that she was expecting.

"Monsieur le Duc wants to see you, *m'mselle*, in the study."

It was a command!

Feeling rather as if the tumbrils were waiting to take her to the guillotine, she walked along the corridor to the Duc's study, which she had discovered was close to the library.

This was one room that she had not yet seen because the children had informed her,

"That is Uncle Etienne's room," and hurried past as if they were afraid that he might pounce out at them.

There was a footman outside the door who opened it for Arletta and she walked in aware as she did so that the Duc was standing at the window, gazing out on the formal garden.

He was silhouetted against the sunlight and she could see that far from being bent or deformed as she had imagined him to be, he was athletically slender and his clothes fitted him as if they had been made in Savile Row.

She could not help feeling that he would be infuriated if he knew what she was thinking, but she had heard her father say,

"All the smartest gentlemen in France have their clothes made in Savile Row in London, while the smartest Englishwomen go to Paris for their gowns!"

She stood just inside the door and she thought the Duc was well aware that she was present.

But he deliberately delayed turning towards her, as if by doing so he asserted his authority and made her feel small and humble,

The footman closed the door behind him, but still the Duc did not turn.

Quite suddenly Arletta stopped feeling apprehensive and afraid.

Instead the pride of the Weirs, which was very much a part of their character, rose so that she felt there was no reason for her to be insulted by anybody, even if he was a Duc.

"You sent for me, *monsieur*?" she said in a quiet clear voice.

She knew, as he turned round, that he was surprised that she should have the audacity to speak first.

She felt that he looked at her deliberately up and down, as if he not only found it hard to believe what she pretended to be but also was looking for something that would enable him to find fault with her.

Slowly, her back very straight, Arletta advanced a little further into the room.

Because the Duc had also begun to move towards her, they met in the middle.

They faced each other and Arletta made a small but graceful curtsey and then informed him,

"I was just about to start David's lesson, *monsieur*, which we do immediately after breakfast until noon."

"Teaching him English!"

The way he spoke made it sound a very reprehensible activity and Arletta replied,

"That, *monsieur*, is my reason for being here."

"I am aware of that," the Duc responded, "but you certainly last night seemed to have made yourself very much at home in my Château!"

There was a note of accusation in his voice that Arletta could not ignore.

"I don't think that is quite the right term, *monsieur*," she answered. "I was not 'making myself at home' in your beautiful ballroom, but stepping back into the past and imagining the room in the Château – as it must have been in the reign of Louis XIV."

She tried to sound brave, but there was a tremor in her voice and, although she was not aware of it, her eyes were apprehensive.

The Duc walked a few paces to stand in front of the impressive marble mantelpiece.

As he turned round, he said abruptly,

"You can sit down, Miss Turner."

"Thank you."

Arletta seated herself on the nearest chair, realising as she did so that its upholstery was a beautiful example of eighteenth century *petit point*.

She felt weak at the knees, but she had no intention of letting the Duc know that he was intimidating her, as she was certain that any other young woman in her position would have felt at this moment.

There was silence until he asked,

"Now, Miss Turner, I am waiting for an explanation as to why the history of the Château and my ancestors should carry you away into realms of fantasy that are unusual for a prosaic Englishwoman."

Arletta heard the note of sarcasm in his voice that seemed to cut like the sharp edge of a knife or as if he was mentally whipping her for her behaviour.

"Even the English, *monsieur*," she replied, "can use their imaginations. I find your Château incredibly beautiful and at the same time very exciting."

"You are not frightened by it or by its inhabitants?" the Duc then enquired.

"To the first part of your question, *monsieur*, the answer is 'no'. To the second I am not yet sure."

Arletta had the idea that at her reply the corners of the Duc's hard mouth twitched a little, as if he was faintly amused.

Then he said,

"Lady Langley, *mademoiselle*, gave you a most fulsome reference as regards both your character and your behaviour. Do you think that is consistent with the way I found you behaving last night?"

"I have already apologised, *monsieur*," Arletta insisted coldly, "for I had no idea since it was so late that in that deserted part of the Château I would be seen by anybody."

The Duc did not speak and after a moment she added,

"I came down from the tower to collect a book from the library. I only intended to savour the – atmosphere of the ballroom and play the piano. My dance was entirely unpremeditated – it just happened!"

"Are you given to having strange things just happen to you, Miss Turner," the Duc asked, "so that, as you have admitted yourself, you are swept away by your imagination? Surely a somewhat precarious pastime for a Governess."

The way he spoke the last words made Arletta certain that he was sneering at her and she replied,

"I cannot believe, *monsieur*, that it is not in many ways a good attribute for a Governess – to have imagination. After all she needs it in order to create by her words a mental picture for her pupils."

"And that is what you do?"

"I try," Arletta replied, "and children respond because they themselves, if they are normal, always have – vivid imaginations that far too often atrophy or are bullied out of them as they grow older."

She spoke positively, thinking that the Duc was using imagination as a weapon to make David and Pauline frightened of what they would find in England or might suffer from the English.

"I understand what you are saying, *mademoiselle*," he remarked, "and I have a feeling that you are at the same time criticising me."

He was more perceptive than Arletta had anticipated and she answered,

"I would not presume, *monsieur*, to do anything of the sort. But I am sure that you are already aware that David is a very imaginative little boy and very perceptive. Perhaps it comes from living here in this Château or perhaps it is merely because being an orphan he has no one he can turn to – and has already learnt to rely on himself."

As she spoke, she knew that she had succeeded in surprising the Duc and so she went on,

"Imagination for all of us can be very wonderful and something that leads, inspires and guides us. It can also be dangerous, frightening and in many cases restricting."

The Duc stared at her.

And then he said,

"Again I think, Miss Turner, that you are speaking directly to me and that your words have a *double entendre*."

"If you think that, *monsieur*, I can only apologise once again. I am concerned only with David and with any reaction he might have to anything I teach him or to – anything he – hears."

She wondered as she spoke whether she had gone too far.

She suddenly had the frightening feeling that the Duc might consider it an impertinence and make it an excuse to be rid of her.

Instead he said,

"I find it hard to believe, Miss Turner, seeing how young you look, that you have had a great experience of teaching. And yet you talk as if you have studied psychology for many years and concerned yourself with matters that are certainly not part of the usual teacher's curriculum."

"I am honoured, *monsieur*, that you should think so."

There was silence and she felt that the Duc was waiting for her to say more.

Then, realising that the conversation had somehow come to an abrupt end, he said,

"I feel, Miss Turner, having spoken to you, that I can leave David's education in English in your hands. But may I suggest that, when he goes to school in your country, he will need plenty of practical common sense rather than airy-fairy fantasies that cannot in any way be substantiated."

"There I agree with you, *monsieur*, and may I say that I feel it important for David and Pauline for that matter to have the companionship of children of their own age."

"Why?"

The question was sharp.

"Because, *monsieur*, it is unnatural for children to be brought up only with grown-ups to talk to. It makes them old beyond their years and it certainly gives rise to those fantasies – that you speak about so scathingly."

She thought that the Duc's eyes flashed at the way that she had answered him, but he replied, drawling the words a little as if to make them more impressive,

"French children are content to be with their families."

"Of course, I am aware of that, *monsieur*, but their families are usually larger than just David and Pauline in the Château."

As she finished speaking, she wondered what the Duc would say and she added,

"If you had children, David would have had a number of cousins to play with and the same might apply to Comte Jacques."

As if the Duc had nothing more to say, he commented abruptly,

"I must not keep you any longer from David and his lessons, Miss Turner. I am only hoping that he will profit by them."

Arletta rose to her feet.

"That is what I am hoping too, *monsieur*. I am very eager that he should look forward to going to Eton and that he will be happy there as his father was."

She thought that she saw an expression of scorn on the Duc's face and went on,

"For most boys, Eton with its games, its excellent education and its comradeship is a great experience that lays a foundation for them in later life that they never forget."

She paused and then said positively,

"I am convinced that David will not only find Eton very enjoyable but he will find there the companionship he needs urgently – even though he is not yet aware of it."

She did not wait for the Duc to reply but merely curtseyed and walked towards the door.

As she reached it, he called out,

"Inform David that he can ride with me after luncheon."

"I will tell him, *monsieur*."

Arletta went from the room and, when she was outside and the door was closed behind her, she drew a deep breath.

After duelling with the Duc in words, knowing that in a way it was a confrontation between them, she felt as if it was hard to breathe.

She had expected that it would be difficult to talk to him, but the words had seemed to come to her lips as if somebody else had put them there.

Now she had the feeling that she had surprised the Duc and had a great deal to think about.

'Why was I not brave enough to ask him to stop poisoning a small boy's mind not only against Eton but against his own country?' she asked herself.

Then she comforted herself that she had not done badly for a first encounter and, what was more, as the Duc had not sacked her, there was likely to be another opportunity.

As she reached the schoolroom, David gave a cry of delight and jumped up from the table of soldiers where he had been sitting.

"You are all right?" he asked. "Uncle Etienne was not disagreeable to you?"

"No, I am all right," Arletta replied. "And now let's continue with your lesson. You should have written the essay I set you yesterday instead of playing with your soldiers."

"I was too worried in case Uncle Etienne sent you away."

"Why should you think – he would do so?"

"Because you are English and because, when he came back last night, you were playing the piano in the ballroom."

"How do you know that?" Arletta gasped.

"I heard Uncle Etienne's valet, who came back with him, telling one of the servants that, as they walked up to his bedroom, they heard music and Uncle Etienne went to see where it came from. Were you not frightened being in that part of the Château in the middle of the night?"

"It was not quite the middle of the night for you had only just gone to bed," Arletta pointed out. "As I told you before, David, I am not frightened of ghosts, which I think are just tales to frighten the foolish and, as I did not know that your uncle was returning, I did not expect anybody to hear me – playing the piano."

"If you had asked me, I would have come with you," he said boastfully.

"That is very sweet of you, David, but I was just thinking how beautiful the ballroom was and I wanted to hear the music of a Strauss waltz being played in it."

She tried to make light of what had happened, being certain that as soon as she had been discovered, the story had run through the Château like wildfire.

"I think you are very brave," David smiled, "and I am quite certain that none of the servants would have dared to go to the ballroom alone."

He paused and then he added eagerly,

"How did you light the candles on the chandelier?"

"I will tell you all about it later," she stipulated firmly.

Arletta told herself that she was right. The story of her behaviour was being gossiped about from the Duchesse down to the lowest scullier.

"Now we have to do our lessons."

"Uncle Etienne did not tell you that we were to stop them?"

"No, of course not," Arletta answered. "He knew that I was coming here to teach you and I think, David, you are making your uncle into a monster, a dragon or an ogre, whichever you like, just because you have nothing else to talk about."

"People talk about him because they are frightened of him and everybody says that he killed his wife!"

"If that is true, he would have – been guillotined!" Arletta answered sharply.

"Somebody pushed her over the battlements," David said in a low voice, "and there was no one else there except for Uncle Etienne. Everybody says that they hated each other and quarrelled all the time."

Arletta slapped her hand down on the table.

"I am not going to listen to all this gossip. It is horrid, it is wrong for you and quite frankly I don't believe a word of it!"

David shrugged his shoulders.

"You may not believe it yourself, but everybody in the Château does and then, when the Comtesse died just when she was expecting to marry Uncle Etienne, everybody said he killed her because he no longer wanted her to be his wife."

Arletta sighed.

"If you are going to go on talking such nonsense, David, and saying such wicked things, which I am sure are lies, I am just going to talk French to you and refuse to teach you any more English."

"That is unfair," David objected at once.

"It is you who is being unfair," Arletta retorted. "In England a man is innocent until he is proven guilty. It may be different in France, but all I can say is that in any civilised country, if your uncle had done the wicked things that you are accusing him of, he would have been brought before a Judge and Jury and hanged or guillotined."

"He got away with it because he was so clever!" David persisted.

"If he did – good luck to him!" Arletta said. "Personally I think the whole thing is a lot of rubbish made up by gossiping women who have nothing better to think about."

She spoke angrily because she thought that it was so bad for the small boy to believe such terrible things about one of his relations and to relate them to her almost with glee.

Then, feeling that she was perhaps taking the wrong tack, she said,

"Listen to me, David, this must have all happened a long time ago and I think, because you are very intelligent, you ought to refuse to believe what people are saying about your uncle unless they can prove to you positively without any question of doubt that he is a murderer."

David was intrigued, as she had expected he would be.

"How could they do that?"

"I don't know, but, as I have said, in England a man is innocent until he is proved guilty. When in future people say things about your uncle like that, I suggest you say, 'prove it, prove it, then I will believe you'. That is the only just and the right way for a gentleman to behave and it is the sporting way as well."

"You are right," David murmured after a moment. "Perhaps it's a mistake to believe that it was Uncle Etienne who pushed Aunt Theresa over the battlements. Nobody knows if she cried out for help or if she threw herself over."

"Now that is a very sensible attitude," Arletta approved.

"The Comtesse," David went on, "who was very beautiful, died of poison through taking too much laudanum. They say that Uncle Etienne gave it to her in her coffee."

"She might have put it in herself," Arletta suggested. "They say that she did not want to die and they say that she really wanted to marry him. They say! They say! They will say – anything to make a good story. Again, David, you are not to believe such wicked things unless you can really prove them. Find somebody who actually saw your uncle putting the laudanum into the coffee or who can prove that he bought it especially to do something so wrong."

"I see what you mean," David said slowly after a moment. "A man would not buy laudanum, would he?"

"Laudanum is a drug that some silly women take because they cannot sleep. But I never heard of a man taking it, unless he was wounded and a doctor gave it to him. When my father was in terrible pain, the doctor said that he could have some, but he waved him away and said it was only women who made themselves insensible."

As she spoke, Arletta remembered that she had often wished that her father was not so brave and would allow himself to be doped.

At least it would have given her a little respite from his fault-finding, his swearing and his continual complaining.

She thought that David was puzzling over what she had said and after a moment she proposed,

"Now, shall we forget your uncle and things that happened years ago and try to get on with the future? Every minute that we waste talking about your uncle is a minute off your efficiency when you yourself go to Eton."

David sat himself down at the table and pulled a book towards him.

"Shall I go on translating what we were reading yesterday?" he asked.

"I am listening," Arletta smiled.

When they went to luncheon, she was glad to see that Comte Jacques was there because she thought that he would divert the Duc's attention from herself and the children.

She was right in that Comte Jacques immediately began to talk to the Duc about the estate, his horses and later the current political situation in Paris.

But she was well aware that while he did so he kept looking at her and she felt anxious in case the Duc might notice it.

She could imagine nothing more uncomfortable than that he should think that she had been encouraging the Comte to pay her compliments.

She had not forgotten that the Duchesse had said how Comte Jacques wished to be rid of her.

Rather than annoy the Duc unnecessarily, she spoke to the children in French, at the same time saying as little as possible so as not to appear to be pushing herself forward.

'If I say nothing, I expect he will think I am dull,' she reflected and decided that a Governess's position was a very precarious one when it was not possible to please everybody, least of all one's employer.

*

When luncheon, which had been a delicious meal, was ended, the Duc and David went riding together.

There was a little pang in her heart as Arletta watched them go, wondering if her riding here had come to an end.

Perhaps the Duc would forbid her to ride or else himself always accompany David, which would mean that there would be no reason for her also to be mounted on one of his magnificent horses.

At the same time she was acutely conscious of him sitting like a King at the end of the table.

He was majestic, but he also had such a strong personality do that she felt she had to look at him and listen to him.

'I *hate* him!' she told herself, but knew that it was not true.

She was intrigued and fascinated by the strangest and most amazing man she had ever met.

Having seen them off, she started to walk rather disconsolately back to the schoolroom and in a way was not surprised when she reached it to find that the Comte waiting for her.

Pauline, she knew, was with her *Bonne* and would lie down for an hour before they went into the garden.

There was a smile on the Comte's lips as she entered the room that made Arletta wary.

"I hope, *monsieur*," she said, "that you don't need me for I have some very urgent letters to write."

"Of course I need you," the Comte replied, "and I missed seeing you yesterday, as I hope you missed me."

"I was far too busy," Arletta answered him.

"You cannot pretend that the chatter of two children is enough to satisfy somebody as intelligent as you are. Besides I have so much to say to you."

"I can only reply that it is unfortunate, as I have some letters that must catch the evening post."

"Very well, I will not keep you long," the Comte agreed, "so come and sit down, Miss Turner, as what I have to say is very important."

Reluctantly, with the feeling that there was nothing else she could do without seeming rude, Arletta sat down on a chair and the Comte sat opposite her.

Then, as if he felt that they were too far away from each other, he rose to take a chair next to hers and said as he did so,

"You are very lovely! I cannot understand why you should waste your looks and your brain on anything so mundane and boring as teaching children."

"Actually, I don't find it at all boring," Arletta replied firmly, "but extremely interesting. My problems are not with the children but with the grown-ups."

If she had thought to embarrass him, she was mistaken for he threw back his head and laughed.

"You are very frank, Miss Turner, but that, of course, is such a typically English trait. Although I know that no Englishwoman can accept a compliment gracefully, let me tell you that you are very beautiful and very desirable."

"If that is all you have to say to me, *monsieur*, I am going up to my bedroom to write my letters."

She would have risen from the chair, but the Comte said hastily,

"What I have to say is most important. I want you to consider very very carefully the proposition I am making to you."

"Proposition?" Arletta repeated.

"It is that you should allow me to take you to Paris to show you the gaieties and the amusements of what to me is the most attractive and enchanting City in the whole world."

Arletta looked at him and then the expression in the Comte's eyes answered the question on her lips.

"I cannot believe, *monsieur*," she said quietly, "that you intend to insult me!"

"Do you really think it is an insult that I should want to make you happy, give you beautiful gowns and a great deal of jewellery, none of which will shine as brightly as your eyes?"

"You are insulting me!"

She rose rapidly to her feet as she spoke and the Comte rose as well and insisted,

"Can you be so foolish as not to understand that, if you accept my offer, you will be a sensation in Paris? Every man I introduce you to will be at your feet!"

"And what will that mean?" Arletta asked.

"Fame, success, riches, a position that most women would give the eyes out of their heads for."

"In which case, *monsieur*, I suggest you offer it to them. As far as I am concerned, never in any circumstances, even if I was starving, would I agree to degrade myself by accepting such a proposition!"

"Then let me make it more attractive," the Comte went on, "by telling you how much you excite me, how much I want you and how very happy I could make you."

He drew closer to her as he spoke, but Arletta stepped back.

"Unfortunately, *monsieur,* you do *not* attract me. Therefore, strange though it may seem to you, I would rather be a Governess than your mistress!"

The Comte stretched out his arms, but she evaded him by slipping round the back of the chair.

Swiftly she moved to the door before he could reach her and, as she left the room, she looked back to say,

"The answer, *monsieur*, is definitely and decisively *no!*"

She did not wait for his reply, but pulled the door sharply to and hurried up the twisting stairs to her bedroom.

After locking the door in case he should follow her, she recalled exactly what he had said and thought that it was not only an insult but there was an ulterior motive in his proposition.

David had said that there was something about the Comte that did not ring true and Arletta would have been prepared to swear that she did not really attract him as much as he pretended.

In which case why was he offering to spend so much money on her?

It was a puzzle that made her stand at the window staring out for a long time at the fields and open country stretching away to the great woods.

Just below the window she was looking of was the river.

She stared down at it, thinking that in the past it had been a natural barrier against enemies who had attempted to storm the Château.

'Now the enemies are within,' she mused.

She wondered if the Duc had any idea of how strangely his relatives behaved or what was said about him, according to David, by everybody.

It was frightening, Arletta thought, but there was more to it than that.

She could think now more clearly of how the Duc had looked at luncheon sitting at the top of the table in his Heraldic chair.

He had seemed a Royal figure who ruled over his domain with a hand of iron and fought his enemies in battles when Arletta was certain that he always returned the victor.

Now his adversaries were using a 'whispering campaign' that was far more difficult to combat.

'Can he really have murdered two women?' Arletta asked herself incredulously.

Her instinct told her that the accusation was untrue, although she had nothing positive to go on.

It was obvious that the Duc inspired fear and that he was a dominating figure with a personality that made other people feel small and uncomfortable.

Human nature being what it was, that inevitably would make them dislike him.

But murder was a very different matter and thinking of him, the way he looked and the way he talked and moved, Arletta could not imagine him intriguing to kill and then covering up his crime with an air of aristocratic innocence.

It was something that seemed alien to such a man, although why she should think so, she had no idea.

'There must be some other explanation,' she thought and wished that she could talk to someone other than David about it.

On an impulse which, because she felt perturbed and upset not only by the Duc but by the Comte's suggestion, she thought that she would visit the small Church that she had seen on her arrival just outside the gates of the Château.

She put on a wide-brimmed hat because the sun was hot and went down the stairs cautiously hoping that by this time the Comte would have left the schoolroom.

The door was open and there was no one there.

With a sigh of relief Arletta went on down the passage, which brought her to a side door where there were no footmen in attendance.

She saw no one and let herself out into the courtyard.

Walking quickly just in case she was noticed by the Comte, she passed through the huge gates and out into the small village outside them.

The Church was less than fifty yards away and, when she entered it, she realised how old it was and how beautiful.

The rounded pillars rose up to an arched ceiling and the walls were enormously thick, while the nave was so small that the congregation was obviously quite limited.

Yet because it was so old there was an air of sanctity and faith that Arletta recognised at once.

She knelt down on a pew at the back of the Church and gazed at the altar.

It was very quiet and, because the windows were small and the glass in them very old, there was little light except in the Sanctuary where a few flickering candles had been lit in front of a statue.

Arletta found herself praying that she would be able to help the children and perhaps, although it seemed an extraordinary request, move the shadow of fear from the Château itself.

'It is so beautiful, God, at the Château' she prayed, 'and beauty should mean love and not hatred.'

When she rose from her knees, she had a sudden wish to light a candle, knowing that Roman Catholics believed that, as long as the candle was burning, the prayers they had said would soar upward to Heaven.

She felt in the pocket of her gown and found to her surprise that there was a small coin there.

It was in fact a shilling that she had intended to put on the offertory plate on the last Sunday she went to Church at home, but for some reason she had taken the money instead from her handbag, forgetting what she had in her pocket.

She was sure that the Priest would find a way of changing English coinage into francs.

She put it now in the small iron box and, taking a candle from where they lay at the foot of the statue, she lit it.

'Please listen to my prayers,' she whispered to God as she did so.

She looked up to find that the Saint who she was praying to was Joan of Arc.

She gave a little smile to herself, thinking how inappropriate it was when the Duc was condemning the English for burning her at the stake.

Although she thought now that, wherever she might be, the Saint would be working for friendship between the English and the French to prevent there being any more wars between the two countries.

St. Joan's voices would tell her that they must learn to love each other even though they were so different in so many ways.

'*Grandmère* would understand that,' Arletta thought.

For the first time since she had arrived at the Château she prayed to her French grandmother to help her to understand and help her countrymen.

"They are partly mine too, *Grandmère*," Arletta said and felt almost as if she could see her grandmother's lovely face and white hair as she smiled at her as if in approval.

Having genuflected to the altar, she then left the Church and walked out into the warm sunshine.

As she did so, she saw coming from the Château gates and dressed in his ordinary clothes since he was off duty, the footman Jean who had escorted her to the Duchesse's room.

"You're here, *m'mselle*!" he exclaimed in surprise.

"Yes, I am here, Jean."

"I see you've been to the Church," Jean remarked. "And now you're in the village, you must come with me to see the witch."

"Oh, no, I cannot!" Arletta replied quickly.

"Why not?" he asked. "No other village has a witch as clever at seein' into the future as ours! Come on. I'll take you to her. I've known her all my life. I'm sure she'll be ever so curious about you."

"I – don't think – " Arletta began.

Suddenly she thought that it could be very interesting. She had never met a witch before and, although she recognised that witchcraft and witches had always played a part in French history, she had never imagined that she would have the chance to actually speak to one.

Quite suddenly her hesitation seemed rather foolish and so she agreed,

"All right, Jean, I will come with you, but you will have to lend me some money to give her, for I have nothing with me."

"That's all right," Jean nodded. "I'll pay for you and you can pay me back when you are paid your wages."

"I will pay you back before that, I don't like to be in debt."

Jean laughed.

"Proud, are you, *m'mselle*? I'd always heard you English give yourselves airs!"

He was teasing her and Arletta merely smiled.

She knew that he was not being impertinent, but just friendly and she thought in some unaccountable that way he, like the Château, was very different from what she had expected.

'I might as well be prepared to accept everything,' she told herself, 'even witches!'

CHAPTER FIVE

The cottage that Jean took her to was very small with a low doorway that he had to bend his head under.

Inside it seemed dark, until, as Arletta's eyes adjusted themselves, she saw sitting in front of the fire, although it was a warm day, a very old woman.

She was wrapped in a dark shawl and her thin hair, which was grey streaked with white, was pinned back at the nape of her withered old neck.

She had strong features with a hooked nose, which made Arletta think that perhaps it was the way she looked more than anything else that had made her a witch.

"I've brought a client for you, Granny," Jean started and the old woman looked up at him quizzically.

"Who is it?" she asked.

Arletta drew nearer and saw that the witch had cataracts over both her eyes, which must make her completely blind.

"I am new to the village," Arletta told her quietly, "and Jean thought that I should meet you, the most important inhabitant here."

The witch chuckled.

"Is that what he said? Well, some people find me important and some are frightened of me."

"I am not frightened."

Jean opened the old witch's hand and put a silver coin into it, saying as he did so,

"You tell the lady all about herself, Granny. I expect, as she's very pretty, you'll find something excitin' for her in the future."

Having spoken, he grinned at Arletta and then went out of the cottage, shutting the door behind him.

There seemed when he had gone to be a strange silence almost, Arletta thought, as if the old woman in front of her had moved into another world.

Arletta sat down opposite her and did not speak and after a few minutes the witch began,

"You're from overseas and you're hidin' somethin' about yourself."

Nervously Arletta looked back just to be certain that Jean was not listening to what was being said.

The door was, however, fast shut and the witch went on.

"I see you puzzling, worrying and afraid. There's danger, real danger! I see *blood*!"

Arletta drew in her breath.

Still she did not speak and after a moment the old witch continued,

"Beware, be ready and protect yourself. When the trouble that will happen to you comes, you must rely on yourself. Remember that – I told you so."

Her voice seemed to die away and, as she apparently had no more to say, Arletta said gently,

"I will remember what you have told me, but it sounds rather a dismal picture."

"Some people are winners," the witch observed after a moment, "and *you* are one."

"Thank you," Arletta replied, "but I am not certain what race I want to win."

The old woman chortled.

"The race of life, my dear, and we're all competin' in that!"

"You really think I am a winner?"

"You will win," the witch emphasised.

Then, as if she wanted Arletta to be sure that she had finished, she lay back in her chair and closed her eyes.

Arletta looked at her for a moment, longing to know more and wondering if she dared ask her about the Duc, but realised that this was impossible.

Then she said once again,

"Thank you," and rose to her feet.

The old witch did not reply and Arletta went out of the cottage to find Jean leaning against a tree and waiting for her.

"Was she any good?" he asked. "What did she tell you?"

"It was rather gloomy," Arletta answered. "She said that there would be trouble, but she did say that I was a winner."

"I'm sure that's true and you've cheered us all up, *m'mselle*, in the Château just because we can look at you."

Arletta gave a little laugh, but she did not reply.

She thought that it would be a mistake to be too familiar about herself to Jean, who she was quite certain was a Don Juan in the village.

She therefore held out her hand, saying,

"Thank you very much, Jean, for being so kind to me. I will give you back the money that you lent me the next time you come to the schoolroom."

"That's all right," Jean smiled.

He realised that Arletta did not wish him to accompany her any further and he therefore touched his cap and walked away down the narrow street while Arletta went back to the Château.

She had just walked into the hall and was about to go up the stairs when Comte Jacques appeared.

"Miss Turner!" he called out. "I want to speak to you."

"I am going to the schoolroom."

"Very well, I will come with you."

There was nothing she could do to stop him and they walked in silence along the corridor that led to the tower.

When they entered the schoolroom, Arletta hoped that Pauline would be there, having finished her rest.

But the room was empty.

She took off her hat and started to tidy some books that had been strewn on the table in the middle of the room.

The Comte closed the door and stood looking at her before he asked,

"Have you considered the suggestion I put to you yesterday?"

"I gave you my answer at the time," Arletta replied coldly, "and it is still 'no'!"

"Women invariably change their minds."

"That may be true of some women, but I have no intention of changing mine. Quite frankly, *monsieur*, as I consider what you said to me to be insulting, I do not wish you to refer to it again."

"Can you really be so foolish?" he asked. "You know that you would enjoy Paris and all the amusing things that I can show you, apart from the fact that I will teach you about love."

There was a note in his voice that Arletta realised was dangerous and she replied quickly,

"It is time for me to give Pauline her lesson in English, so if you have nothing sensible to say, *monsieur*, I must ask you to leave."

The Comte laughed softly and came towards her.

He moved swiftly and had his arms around her before she had a chance to realise what had happened.

She gave a cry of protest and then struggled against him. As he drew her closer in spite of her efforts, she felt how strong he was and that he intended to kiss her.

"I want you," he breathed. "Whatever you feel about me is of little consequence because I want you."

Now there was a note in his voice that told her that he was not pretending and that she genuinely excited him.

And there was a fire in his eyes that was unmistakable.

"Let me go!" she cried out, pushing him away from her with both her hands on his chest, knowing how ineffectual she was being, as his lips were almost touching hers.

She turned her head frantically first one way and then the other to try to avoid him.

She felt his mouth warm and insistent against her cheek.

Then, as she gave another cry, knowing that she was completely helpless, the door opened and as the Comte released her, Pauline came running in.

"I am late, *m'mselle*," she cried, "but I fell asleep and *ma Bonne* did not wake me."

Breathless and, feeling her heart beating in an agitated manner, Arletta managed to answer.

"You are not too late – for your lesson – and as it is such a lovely afternoon – we will go into the garden."

She realised that her voice was coming in jerks as she spoke, but Pauline did not seem to notice.

Instead she was looking at the Comte and said,

"I don't want you, Cousin Jacques, to listen to my lessons. You will laugh when I make mistakes."

"I don't laugh at Mademoiselle Turner," he told her.

His eyes were on Arletta and she knew that instead of being angry he was amused by what had happened.

He was obviously confident that she would eventually capitulate and do what he asked of her.

Because she felt that she could not bear to be near him for another moment, she picked up her hat from where she had put it on a chair and then said to Pauline,

"Come along, let's go into the garden just as we are and you can tell me the names – of the flowers and the birds in English."

"I can remember some of them, *mademoiselle*."

Pauline slipped her hand into Arletta's as she spoke and, without either of them giving another glance at the Comte, they went out of the schoolroom and down the stairs towards the door that led into the garden.

In the sunshine, as she began to teach Pauline, Arletta felt her agitation subside.

At the same time she was aware that, if this was the danger that the witch had spoken about, it was something that would happen again and again.

She wondered how she could possibly persuade the Comte to leave her alone and even for one moment contemplated speaking to the Duc.

Then she was sure that, as he hated her for being English, he would be certain that it was her fault and that she had encouraged the Comte to behave so insultingly.

'What can I do, *what can I do?*' she asked herself desperately.

It was a question that was at the back of her mind all the afternoon as they wandered round the beautiful gardens.

They sat at length on a stone seat beneath a statue of Aphrodite.

Looking back at the Château silhouetted against a cloudless blue sky, Arletta felt that it was so lovely that it was wrong for so many conflicting and unpleasant emotions to be harboured inside it.

How could anybody living amid such beauty have nothing but hatred in their hearts?

She must have been silent for some minutes because Pauline became bored and jumped up from her side to run towards the fountain.

Arletta saw that she was watching the goldfish swimming in and out of the water lily leaves in the stone bowl.

She thought as she looked at the child with the water rising up behind her that this was another picture that, as far as she was concerned, would be always unforgettable.

Then to her astonishment a voice came from behind her,

"What are you thinking about, Miss Turner?"

She looked up to see that it was the Duc.

He had obviously just come back from riding for he was wearing his riding breeches and jacket.

She would have risen, but he said, "no, don't get up," and sat down beside her.

"If you are back, *monsieur*," she said, "I should go to find David."

"David wanted to practise over the smaller jumps in what I call my riding school," the Duc replied. "I have left my Head Groom with him, so he does not require your attention at present."

As he spoke in his dry rather cynical manner, he made Arletta feel as if she was being needlessly fussy.

She turned her head away to look again at Pauline by the fountain.

"I would be interested to know, Miss Turner, what you think of my Château," the Duc enquired.

Arletta smiled,

"I was thinking just a minute ago, *monsieur*, that it is so beautiful that everybody who looks at it and lives in it should think only of love and not anything wrong or evil."

"Love is something that most women are mainly concerned with," the Duc observed cynically.

"I don't mean that – kind of love," Arletta said sharply. "I mean the love of beauty that one finds in the countryside, in your garden and should be in a building that is so old and so perfectly preserved."

"I stand corrected!"

Arletta knew that he was being sarcastic and she responded,

"Perhaps you will think it very impertinent of me, *monsieur*, but while you are entitled to be cynical if you wish, it is wrong for children and quite frankly I am worried in case, being orphans, David and Pauline should grow up with the wrong ideas about life."

She felt as she spoke that she was being extremely brave in telling the Duc the truth.

But she told herself that perhaps it would make him think that he should not show his feelings so obviously.

The Duc looked at her quizzically before he remarked,

"I have a feeling, Miss Turner, that even for an Englishwoman you are a very unusual type of Governess."

"I think that all Governesses are intimately concerned with their charges and it is not just a question of teaching lessons but also teaching them about life."

"And that is a subject that you know a great deal about?" the Duc remarked and once again he was being sarcastic.

"I suppose the truth is," Arletta replied, "that I know very little and that is why I still, *monsieur*, have illusions and ideals and I have no wish to lose them here."

She knew as she spoke that she had surprised him and he said,

"You have made your point, Miss Turner. And I shall certainly think over what you have said to me."

He rose abruptly from the stone seat and, as he walked away, Arletta wondered if she had offended him and perhaps she had made a mistake in saying so much.

She thought now that it was time they returned to the Château and the schoolroom and she therefore called Pauline and they went back through the formal garden with the little girl telling her about the goldfish as they went.

They walked in through the garden door and, as they reached the passage that led up to the schoolroom, she saw that the Comte was waiting for them.

As she had no wish to speak to him, Pauline ran ahead up the steps to the tower.

When Arletta would have followed her, the Comte seized her wrist and stopped her.

"What was my cousin saying to you?" he demanded fiercely.

Arletta, who had been expecting him to ask something very different, looked at him in surprise.

"Does it matter?"

"I want to know!"

There was something fierce about the way that the Comte spoke and the expression in his eyes.

"It was not very interesting," Arletta said hastely. "He was just explaining that David had not returned to the schoolroom – but was practising over the jumps."

"Is that all?" the Comte enquired.

"That is all of – any consequence."

As she spoke, Arletta twisted her wrist free of his hand and walked away.

She had a strong feeling that he was watching her until she disappeared through the schoolroom door.

She could not believe that he was jealous and yet there was something sharp about his questions that told her he was perturbed because the Duc had spoken to her in the garden.

'He is certainly very tiresome,' she told herself.

Then she wondered once again how she could persuade him to leave her alone.

*

That evening to Arletta's surprise there were several guests for dinner.

Among them were the Marquis and Marquise de Vasson, who lived, Arletta learnt, about six miles from the Château.

The Marquise de Vasson was an extremely beautiful woman who was just at the age when her youth was a little behind her and middle age just a few years ahead.

She sat on the Duc's right and, because Arletta found it fascinating to watch the French visitors, she was quite certain before dinner ended that the Duc and the Marquise had at one time been very close to each other.

It was obvious that she was still attracted to him and used every wile to hold his interest and was perhaps tring to revive the flame that had burnt itself out.

Arletta had no idea why she should know these things.

Yet, although she had expected a Frenchwoman to be flirtatious when she was with an attractive man, she knew instinctively with a perception that she was not aware she possessed that the Marquise was still infatuated by the Duc.

He spoke to her in his dry manner and there was nothing in his expression or in his half-closed eyes to make Arletta think that his feelings were in any way unusual.

And yet she knew, almost as if somebody had told her, that at one time he had felt very differently.

The Marquis was a much older man with white hair, slightly deaf, and who talked incessantly and extremely boringly on obscure subjects that were not particularly interesting to anyone else at the table.

The Comte had on either side of him two middle-aged but good-looking women, who were very eager to entertain him.

Arletta realised that he was bored and was aware that his eyes kept straying down the table to where she was sitting with the children.

That was also true of another man in the party, the husband of one of the women beside the Comte.

Arletta was certain that he was the local roué, the type of elderly man who would pursue any young girl if he had the chance.

He had singled her out before dinner when the children had been taken to the salon to meet the Duc's guests.

She noted that David bowed, French fashion, over the ladies' hands and Pauline dropped little curtseys to everybody.

Arletta stood in the background, remembering how her own Governess had behaved when she was a child, but to her surprise the Duc had brought her forward and introduced her whilst saying,

"I know you will be astonished to see that I have an Englishwoman in the Château, but David and Pauline's aunt, Lady Langley, who was here recently, insisted that they should learn English, which is a subject, as you are well aware, I have no intention of teaching them myself!"

There was laughter at this and the Marquise put her hand on his arm and said in a voice that was full of meaning,

"Why should you, my dear Duc, teach anything but the art that you are supreme and unchallenged in?"

"You flatter me," the Duc responded dryly and continued to introduce Arletta to his guests.

She had not made the mistake of dressing up when she heard that there was to be a dinner party.

Instead she had worn the most severe evening gown she possessed, which actually was very becoming and had deliberately arranged her hair in a way that she thought was most appropriate for a Governess.

However, because it waved naturally, no matter how tightly she dragged it back, in a few minutes it was in waves against her oval forehead and because her hair was so long it was impossible to wear it in a bun and so she arranged it in a chignon at the back of her head.

'Nobody will notice me,' she told herself, 'and all I have to do is to look neat and tidy.'

But as Jane had mentioned, Arletta made everything she wore seem a perfect frame for her figure and there was nothing she could do to alter her large eyes that dominated her small pointed face.

"And are you a very strict Governess?" the old roué asked her in a low voice so that he could not be overheard.

"I try to be," Arletta replied.

"I think, *mademoiselle*," he went on, "your lips were not made for speaking English to the Duc's nephew and niece but for kisses!"

To Arletta's annoyance she found herself blushing before she turned away to speak to Pauline.

She was well aware during dinner that the roué was watching her from the other side of the table.

In fact wherever she looked she encountered either his eyes or the Comte's.

When dinner finally came to an end, she was relieved to be able to take Pauline upstairs, although David stayed with the guests a little longer.

Then, just as Arletta was thinking that she would go to bed, he came into the schoolroom and, when he saw her smile, he said,

"They talked about you when you had left, *mademoiselle*."

"What did they say?" Arletta enquired.

"They all commented that you were too young and too pretty to be a Governess! The Marquise told Uncle Etienne that she would find somebody better than you to teach us."

"And what did your uncle reply to that?"

"I spoke first," David replied, "and I told the Marquise that you were a really good Governess and I had learnt a lot of English and I had no wish to have anybody else to teach me."

Arletta was touched.

"That was very sweet of you, David."

"They all laughed at me," David added a little resentfully, "and the fat man with the red face said, 'you are quite right, my boy, you keep her while you have the chance'."

"Thank you," Arletta smiled at him. "And now as it is so late you had better go to bed otherwise we shall waste time in the morning and that would be a mistake."

"My English is better, is it not, *mademoiselle*?" David asked anxiously.

"You have worked very hard and I am very proud of you," Arletta answered. "I do not believe that anybody could have learnt English faster than you have, but there is still a great deal more to do."

"I know," David replied, "and before I go to sleep I talk to myself in English and I try to think in it too."

"That is very very sensible of you."

For the first time since she had been in the Château she bent her head and kissed him.

To her surprise he put his arms around her and gave her a hug.

"I like being with you, *mademoiselle*," he murmured.

She had the feeling that he was missing his mother and hugged him back before she answered,

"Good night, David, sleep well and happy dreams."

"I should say that to you in case the ghosts come to haunt you."

"I doubt if they will."

Arletta smiled and went upstairs to her bedroom in the tower.

The maid had left a small oil lamp burning by her bed, which was turned low, and she crossed the room to turn it up before she walked back to the door to lock it.

It was then to her surprise that she found the key that had been there the night before and every night since she had come to the Château was no longer in the lock.

She thought that it must have fallen out and then searched on the floor, but there was no sign of it.

Then suddenly she was nervous.

Suppose the Comte, after what he had said, came to her room?

She could hardly believe that he would do such a thing and yet the way he had spoken when he tried to kiss her had been frightening.

Then she remembered the way that he had questioned her about the Duc and she thought that he must be jealous.

If he came late at night, there would be no one to hear her if she screamed, except for the children and she was certain that they slept soundly.

She suddenly felt very young and helpless and knew that Jane had been right when she had warned her against Frenchmen.

It seemed inconceivable that the Comte could behave in such a dishonourable way to a woman who was employed by his cousin.

Yet she had the inescapable feeling that the explanation of her key having vanished was that he had taken it.

'What shall I do? What shall I do?' she asked herself.

She felt that she must ask somebody to help her, but she knew that really the only person she could appeal to was the Duc and that was impossible.

She thought of going to find the housekeeper and asking if she could change her room and then remembered how everybody gossiped in the Château.

If she said anything about a missing key, it would undoubtedly make the staff suspicious.

Speculation as to who had taken it would run from room to room like wildfire and would certainly reach the Duchesse's ears.

'What shall I do?' she asked again.

She decided that the Comte was far more frightening than any ghost could ever be.

Suddenly she had an idea.

The first day when David had taken her round the Château he had shown her the Armoury.

She had seen the cannon, the bows and arrows and the old muskets that had been used by the private Army of the Ducs de Sauterre.

But also in the huge room, which was at the bottom of one of the towers, there had been a cabinet where was displayed a number of smaller weapons.

"Some of these," David explained, "were given as presents to various Ducs by Kings, Princes, Sultans and Sheiks."

Because the small boy had been in a hurry to show Arletta everything in the Armoury, she had time for only a perfunctory glance at the cabinet and what it contained.

Now she remembered that she had noticed a small revolver set with jewels.

"What is that?" she had asked David, attracted by the glittering stones.

He did not answer. He had moved away, but she saw written on a card the date that it had been presented to the then Duc by the Czar of Russia.

Because she was sure that it was the only protection that might help her now, she ran as quickly as she could down the twisting staircase of the tower.

She then found her way with some difficulty to the Armoury.

It was on the other side of the Château and, while some of the rooms were lit by gas, the oldest part had either oil lamps or candles.

When she came to the end of a long passage, where the candles were in sconces, there was only darkness and she realised that she would have to carry one with her.

It was the only light available to guide her the rest of the way to the Armoury.

To her relief the door was not locked and she walked in, feeling the cold from the unplastered walls and aware that it was what the children would have called 'creepy' because the ceiling was so high and everything was dark and still.

She remembered where the cabinet was situated and walked across the stone floor to it.

It was not locked. She raised the lid and looked down at the miscellaneous collection of swords, daggers and duelling pistols.

It was quite easy to see what she was looking for because the amethysts that the handle of the revolver was studded with and the small diamonds surrounding them flashed in the candlelight.

Arletta put down the candle and lifted the revolver.

She had often fired not only her father's shotgun but also his revolver, which was not very up to date.

He had also been amused when she had tried firing the duelling pistols that had belonged to her great-grandfather. He was reputed to have been such a dashing buck that he had fought innumerable duels when King George IV was the Prince of Wales.

The revolver might be elaborately decorated, but it appeared to Arletta to be quite a serviceable weapon.

She also saw to her relief that there was a little pile of bullets, which had been dipped in gold, lying beside it.

She picked them all up and, carrying them and the revolver in one hand and the candle in the other, started back on the somewhat tortuous journey to the tower occupied by her and the children.

When she reached the lit part of the long corridor, she put the candle back in the sconce that she had taken it from.

Then, as she walked on, she heard voices and stopped.

Someone was coming and quickly she hid herself in the shadows of a large doorway.

She then realised that what she had heard were the voices of some of the guests. They were leaving the salon that they had gone into after dinner and she wondered why.

Then, as they drew nearer, she realised that the two people approaching her down the passage were the Duc and the Marquise.

She pressed herself even further into the darkness of the doorway where she had hidden and then, afraid that she might be seen, she swiftly turned the handle of the door behind her and slipped into the room.

She left the door slightly ajar and through the crack she saw the Duc and the Marquise pass down the corridor, her arm linked in his.

"I have missed you, Etienne," Arletta heard the Marquise say. "How can you make me live without seeing you? It is cruel, unbelievably cruel!"

"People are talking about us, Justine," the Duc replied, "and you know that is a mistake from your point of view."

"It may be a mistake, but I love you," the Marquise replied and Arletta heard the pain in her voice.

They moved on and she could no longer hear what they said.

Then she guessed that they were going to look at the small aviary, which was a little further along the passage and which she had passed without realising it. There were quite a number of small unusual birds in it and Pauline loved them all.

Arletta supposed that the Marquise had made her desire to view the aviary an excuse to take the Duc away from his other guests.

For some reason that she could not understand, she felt it painful to realise that the Duc was listening to the lovely woman on his arm.

When she knew that they were no longer in the corridor, she sped as quickly as she could to her bedroom without seeing anyone else.

She put the revolver down on the dressing table and recognised, now that she had the protection of it, that she was no longer helpless.

It seemed to her that, when she held it in her hands, she could think more clearly and there was no reason to be in a panic.

As she loaded the revolver, she realised that the bullets were so small that they could not kill a man unless he was struck in a very vulnerable place.

But it would most certainly be extremely painful if a bullet pierced someone's arm or leg.

'Now I feel safe,' she told herself and, putting the revolver down, started to move the furniture in the room in front of the door.

She found a chair that was high enough to insert under the handle, but which alone, she was aware, might be pushed aside if any great force was exerted against it.

Then she moved a chest of drawers with some difficulty, because it was heavy, against the rest of the door.

'That will certainly keep out the Comte,' she thought with satisfaction.

In the meantime, having undressed and climbed into bed, she put the small revolver under her pillow, feeling quite proud of herself for being so self-sufficient.

"The witch was right," she said aloud, "I shall win this battle."

Then she remembered with a little feeling of horror that the old woman had seen blood.

'Once he knows I have a revolver,' she reasoned to herself, 'he will not be such a fool as to risk my shooting him.'

It was a frightening thought, but, because she was very tired and it had been a hot day, she fell asleep at once.

*

When Arletta awoke, it was to find that the sun was streaming through the curtains of the windows and it was morning.

She sat up in bed and, looking across at the furniture she had piled in front of the door, she wondered if the Comte had tried to come to her as she had feared that he might.

She had the feeling that he had done so, but, on finding the door barred, had not risked making a noise by trying to force it open.

She could not be sure, she only knew that she had slept without being disturbed and that was more important than anything else.

She put the furniture back in its usual places before the maid came to call her.

When she was dressed, she went downstairs with the children to the breakfast room.

She wondered if when she saw the Comte she would be able to tell if he had come to her bedroom or not.

To her surprise, however, there was no sign of him or the Duc and the servants explained that the Comte had left early to spend the day with friends and the Duc as usual had gone riding.

The morning passed in a quiet normal fashion with David having his lessons until to Arletta's joy they went riding.

She thought as she rode one of the most magnificent horses she had ever known that she was so happy that it was worth any difficulties, even those occasioned by the Comte, to be at the Château and have so many privileges.

They had ridden through the Park and Arletta was thinking that it was time they returned home for luncheon when she saw a magnificent figure on a horse coming towards them and saw that it was the Duc.

"Oh, here comes Uncle Etienne," David said in a disagreeable tone of voice, "We don't want him finding fault with us."

"Perhaps he will praise us," Arletta suggested. "You know, David, he has been very kind and good-tempered about you having an English Governess."

"That is true," David agreed. "I thought he would make far more fuss about it."

"Be nice to him," Arletta suggested quickly as the Duc reached them.

"Good morning, Uncle Etienne," David said as the Duc raised his hat to Arletta. "Can I show you how fast I can go now on Le Roi? It's the biggest horse I have ever ridden."

"I shall be interested to see your progress," the Duc answered.

David rode towards the long flat piece of land where the Duc had just been riding.

Then he touched his horse with his whip and set off at a tremendous pace.

The Duc watched him with a faint smile before he turned to Arletta,

"I suppose we had better follow him, Miss Turner. Have you enjoyed your ride?"

"This is the most wonderful horse I could ever imagine!" Arletta enthused.

"By that I assume you ride in your dreams."

"Only when I can be on a horse as marvellous as this."

She thought that he was amused by her reply, but he did not speak as they were now riding a little more swiftly towards the end of the field where David was waiting for them.

As they trotted side by side, the Duc remarked,

"I see you have been well taught."

"My father was very insistent that I should ride correctly."

"I am sure that he was not disappointed in you."

It was almost a compliment and Arletta looked at him with laughter in her eyes as she said,

"I was thinking just before you joined us that to have horses like this to ride would make up for all the other disappointments and problems in life."

"Have you many problems?" the Duc enquired and Arletta, remembering the Comte, looked away from him.

"A – few."

"Perhaps I could solve them for you."

Arletta was so surprised at the suggestion that she stared at him in astonishment.

Then she said quickly,

"No, no! Of course not. I have to learn to look after myself and that is what the witch told me – I must do."

"The witch?" the Duc questioned her at once. "Do you mean to tell me that you have been to see that old charlatan?"

He spoke angrily and Arletta felt that she had been indiscreet.

But by that time they had reached David and there was no need for her to say anything more.

"That was good, was it not, Uncle Etienne?" the small boy asked.

"Very good!" the Duc exclaimed. "I know if your mother had been here, she would have been very proud of you."

Then, without saying anymore, he rode off and left them.

For a moment Arletta and David just sat on their horses watching him go.

Then David said,

"Did you hear what he said, *mademoiselle?* He praised me and that is something he has never done before!"

CHAPTER SIX

There was only the Duc at luncheon and it was a great relief to Arletta that the Comte was not present.

To her surprise the Duc seemed to be in a very good temper and told interesting stories about the Château and she thought for the moment at any rate that he had ceased hating her.

He was pleasant too to the children and did not sneer at them or speak disparagingly about their learning English.

"What are you going to do this afternoon?" he asked as luncheon finished.

There was a little pause before Arletta replied,

"I had hoped, *monsieur*, that David and I might go riding again as it is such a lovely day, but, of course, if you think it is too much, we could easily do something else."

"I think it is an excellent idea if you keep under the trees where it is cool," the Duc advised, "and, as I don't think that you have visited one of the more interesting of my woods, I will show you the way."

Arletta was surprised by the offer but accepted gratefully.

He led her and David in a different direction from the one they had taken before and they entered a wood where the trees were much more mature.

She found it fascinating, especially as the Duc pointed out and named the different birds that they saw.

He also seemed to be in such a good temper that David chattered away to him without any sign of the fear and dislike that he had shown previously.

In the very centre of the wood there was a very old Chapel that had been built almost at the same time as the original Château.

It was hardly ever used, the Duc informed her, but when they dismounted and went inside Arletta felt as if the same sanctity she had felt in the village Church was present.

All the furnishings had been taken away, leaving only the bare stones of its walls. Birds had nested in the rafters and there were lizards running over the walls.

Yet she thought for the animals of the forest at any rate it was still a place where they could find sanctuary from hunters or predators.

She did not say so aloud, but, as if the Duc could read her thoughts, he said,

"I used to think when I was a boy that the animals that were wounded by sportsmen or perhaps by some other animal came here and the spirits of the monks who once officiated looked after them. Now you are thinking the same as me."

"How did you know what – I was thinking?" Arletta questioned.

He smiled enigmatically and then added,

"Your eyes are very revealing, *mademoiselle!*"

She felt shy and, when they rode on again, she left David to talk to his uncle while she at first listened and then joined in the conversation.

At the same time she was sure with a feeling of relief that the Duc's hatred for her as an Englishwoman was not as intense as it had been when she had first arrived.

She hoped now for the children's sake that there would be a happier atmosphere at the Château than she had sensed at first.

'He has such a strong personality,' she reflected. 'He must use it to inspire the people around him.'

And, as she heard the Duc's deep voice answering one of David's questions, she added to herself,

'He should be the leader – '

There was a little pause and a voice inside her mind that she could not control added – *with love.*

When they returned and entered the hall, a footman informed Arletta that the Duchesse wished to see her.

She had known for the last two days that the Duchesse had been unwell and had not wanted to see anybody.

When she had changed her riding habit for one of her simple gowns, a footman escorted her to the Duchesse's apartments.

Today she was looking even more fantastic, Arletta thought, wearing a ruby necklace round her throat, huge rubies in her ears and the same stones round her wrists and on her fingers.

As Arletta came nearer to the bed, the Duchesse gazed at her with the shrewd searching expression in her eyes that she had noticed before.

"Come and tell me what you are up to, young woman," she demanded. "I hear that Jacques is pursuing you and that you have been out riding with my grandson."

Because Arletta could not help it, she gave a little laugh.

"Why are you laughing?" the Duchesse asked.

"Because, *madame*," Arletta replied, "you know everything that happens in the Château – even though you are confined to your bedroom."

"What else do I have to interest me except for the vagaries and peculiarities of other people," the Duchesse asked.

Arletta did not answer and the Duchesse went on,

"What has Jacques been saying to you? I am told he is pursuing you, but it is unusual for him to interest himself in Governesses. Are you encouraging him?"

"I assure you, *madame*," Arletta answered her coldly, "that I have told Comte Jacques quite positively to leave me alone and I only hope he does so."

"Setting your sights a little higher?" the Duchesse enquired.

"I am setting my sights on making certain that David speaks perfect English by the time he goes to Eton," Arletta replied. "He has made tremendous progress as he is very eager to learn and therefore it is coming easily to him."

"So you think you are a very efficient teacher, do you?" the Duchesse asked.

"I hope so, *madame*."

The Duchesse looked at her as if she was trying to penetrate deeper to below what appeared on the surface.

Then she suggested,

"Tell me more about yourself, *mademoiselle*. I am extremely curious."

"You would find me a very dull subject, *madame*," Arletta answered, "and, if you will excuse me, I need to be with Pauline, who will be feeling neglected as I have been so busy with David all day."

"Any excuse to get away, I suppose," the Duchesse murmured almost to herself. "Never mind, nothing can be hidden forever and sooner or later the truth will out!"

"So I have always been told, *madame*, but if one is not afraid of the truth, why should one worry?"

She curtseyed to the old woman and then, without waiting for her to say anything more, she walked across the room.

She half-expected by the time she reached the door to be called back, but the Duchesse did not speak and with a sense of relief Arletta found herself outside in the corridor.

The old maid was waiting outside for her and she said almost apologetically,

"You mustn't mind anythin' Madame la Duchesse says to you, *mademoiselle*, even though it may seem rude. She's very old and is ill most of the time, but still dislikes being left out of everythin'."

"I can understand," Arletta remarked gently.

"She's worried too," the maid went on, "about the things Comte Jacques tells her about the Duc."

Arletta guessed what these were and she said,

"Perhaps you could persuade Madame that Comte Jacques is not always to be relied upon. If you ask me, I think he is a troublemaker."

She thought as she spoke that she was being indiscreet. But she was quite certain that Comte Jacques was telling the Duchesse stories about the Duc and herself and trying to whitewash his own behaviour, which she considered disgraceful.

'I wish he would go away,' she murmured to herself as she walked back to the tower. 'The place is much happier without him.'

She gave Pauline a short lesson from the books that they had brought from the library while David translated two pages of a history book into English.

When they had finished, he said,

"There is still one place in the Château that you have not yet visited, *mademoiselle*, and that is the dungeons."

"After all the horrid stories I have heard about them, I am not really interested," Arletta answered.

"Why not come with me now?" David suggested. "I am surprised that you have not heard the groans and cries of the prisoners."

"Do you mean the dungeons are under this tower?" Arletta asked him.

"Most of them. There is one that has a trap door, which swings down to leave a huge hole in the floor."

"I have heard about those sorts of traps," Arletta said, "and I think they are very cruel."

"One Duc de Sauterre in the seventeenth century had a crueller trap than anybody else," David continued as if it was something to be proud about. "When he pulled the lever, the victim fell through a trapdoor into a cage that was embedded deep in the bottom of the river where he drowned."

Arletta reckoned that this was against all the rules of war whereby there was always the chance that prisoners could be exchanged or ransomed when the war was over.

The idea of dungeons and traps made her shudder and she commented,

"Don't let us talk about it, David, and quite frankly I don't wish to see your dungeons."

"They are a long way beneath us," David said cheerily, "so there is no reason to think about them unless you hear the ghosts of those who died groaning, as the servants think they do."

"I have not heard or seen any ghosts since I have been here," Arletta stated firmly, "and I am now convinced that all the talk about them is just foolish superstition."

She then proposed that the children should go to the aviary to feed the birds and, as they were delighted to do so, they hurried off down the passage where she had seen the Duc and the Marquise the previous evening.

Although she told herself that it was none of her business, she could not help thinking of the two of them together and the way that the Marquise had insisted to the Duc that she loved him.

As the children ran from cage to cage giving the birds the seeds and fruit they enjoyed, she wondered if, when the Duc made love to a woman, he looked as bored and cynical as he did at other times.

Then she told herself that it was very immodest for her to think about such thoughts.

Yet, because in his own way he was so outstanding and different from any man she had ever seen before, it was impossible not to think about him.

"I would like to have a little bird of my own," Pauline was saying. "I could have it in a cage in the schoolroom and listen to it singing."

"You will have to ask your uncle if you can have one, but I can see no reason why not."

"I am sure Uncle Etienne will say 'no'," Pauline looked worried.

"There is no harm in trying," Arletta replied.

"He was very nice to me today," David volunteered.

"Who was nice to you?" a voice asked from the doorway.

Arletta looked round and felt her heart sink.

Comte Jacques had come into the aviary when she had hoped that they would be free of him for a time.

As if he felt that he had to answer the Comte, David said,

"I was talking about Uncle Etienne."

"Why was he so nice to you?" the Comte enquired.

"Mademoiselle and I went riding with him. He took us to the old Chapel in the wood and it was very interesting."

David spoke almost defiantly, as if he expected the Comte to say that it had been nothing of the sort.

Instead the Comte looked at Arletta in what she thought was a strange manner before he said,

"So my estimable cousin has been pleasant, has he indeed, despite the fact that you are English?"

It was what Arletta had thought herself, but there was no need for Comte Jacques to emphasise it.

It was something he would doubtless talk about to the Duchesse in such a way that she would put a very different construction upon it.

"I think," she said in a cold rather repressive voice, "that Monsieur has accepted that it is essential for David to speak English properly before he goes to an English school."

"And, of course, he is extremely fortunate in having such an attractive, charming and intelligent teacher."

Arletta sighed to herself.

She found it very irritating that the Comte went on paying her compliments and was, she was sure, still expecting to persuade her to accept his invitation to go to Paris.

He naturally had no idea how insulting it was to her, not being the Governess that he thought her to be.

It was something he would never have thought of suggesting if he had known her real identity and he would not have dared to put such a 'proposition', as he called it, to a French girl with a protective family behind her.

"I think it is time we returned to the schoolroom," Arletta turned to the children.

"All right," David agreed.

Pauline was taken reluctantly away from the birds, still repeating that she wanted to have one of her very own.

The Comte did not speak as Arletta, holding Pauline by the hand, left the aviary.

Yet she knew that he was watching her and she could feel his eyes almost as if they were boring their way through her white skin.

'He is increasingly tiresome and I have no wish to have anything more to do with him,' she told herself.

Equally she recalled the revolver that she had locked away in a drawer in her bedroom and knew how glad she was to have it.

There was no one else for dinner except the Comte and once again the Duc was pleasant and, Arletta thought, exceptionally interesting.

She found herself discussing with him the pictures in the Château and realised that he was surprised she knew so much about art.

It was with difficulty that she refrained from telling him that in Weir House there was a collection of family portraits that was noted as being one of the finest in the whole of England.

As the Duc had so much to say, the Comte was surprisingly quiet and, when Arletta took Pauline away upstairs, she felt, although she was not sure, that he looked at her resentfully because she had ignored him.

There was certainly an expression in his dark eyes that she did not like.

She knew that once again she would pile the furniture in front of her door and sleep with the little Russian revolver under her pillow.

However, because it had been an active day, she did not lie awake worrying about the Comte or anybody else, but fell asleep soon after she had climbed into her bed.

*

She was dreaming that she was riding a very large horse when suddenly she came back to consciousness aware that something had disturbed her,

Her thoughts immediately went to the Comte and she lay in the darkness listening and wondering if what she had heard was an attempt by the Comte to open the door.

She wondered whether in the morning she should ask the housekeeper for another key or suggest that a bolt be fixed, which would prove just as effective.

She knew exactly what the Duchesse would say and told herself that she could not bear to think of how it would be whispered amongst the staff and how they would look at her speculatively as if it was her fault that the key had disappeared.

'I will manage as I did last night,' she determined.

Actually it had needed a considerable amount of strength to drag the chest of drawers again in front of the door, but it was certainly preferable to knowing that everybody was talking about her.

Now for some seconds there were no more sounds and, thinking that she must have been mistaken, she turned her head sideways on her pillow ready to go back to sleep again.

Then suddenly she heard a cry that was quite different from the sound that she had expected and, although it was not very loud, it was a sound like a shriek of pain.

It flashed through her mind that this came from the ghosts that David had talked about so much and was what she had been told to expect to hear ever since she had slept upstairs in the tower.

Just for a moment a sense of fear seemed to invade her whole body and, as the shriek came again, she closed her eyes as if she was afraid that an apparition would suddenly appear in front of her in the darkness.

Then, as she trembled and was ashamed of the fact, her common sense told her that whatever the servants might say, as a rule ghosts do not make noises or speak.

Now the shriek was repeated and as she listened Arletta was almost certain that it came from some small animal.

The cry grew worse and more persistent and she told herself that it must be a rabbit or a cat that had been caught in a trap.

It was impossible to ignore it, so she sat up in bed and lit the oil lamp, which she had blown out when she was ready to go to sleep.

She realised that the sound came from the West window of her room, which looked out over the fields towards the woods.

Because the cries were continuing and now seemed to Arletta to be even more agonising, she jumped out of bed and opened the window as wide as possible.

She leaned over the sill, which was the thickness of the tower walls, to look out.

The river was directly beneath her on this side of the tower and she knew that there were some trees and shrubs on the other side of it before the open fields.

Now she realised that the sound was coming from directly below her, in fact at the foot of the tower and, although it was impossible to see, she was sure that some animal was caught in a trap.

'Perhaps I could release it,' she reflected.

She realised that the only way to do so would be to go to the bottom of the tower where the dungeons were situated.

'It would be better to wait until morning when it is light,' she told herself.

Then she knew, as the shrieks continued, that it would be impossible for her to sleep knowing that some poor creature was suffering so intensely.

She wondered if it would be possible to find one of the servants and tell them what was happening.

But she had a feeling that they would not be particularly interested as long as it was not a human being who was crying out in such agony.

'I should be sensible and forget it,' she told herself.

But she could not.

Resolutely she first lit the candles on her dressing table and then put on the blue satin negligée that the maid had placed over a chair.

As she buttoned it down the front, Arletta realised that it had a pretty lace-trimmed pocket on one side of it.

She thought that if she could see the animal in the trap from one of the windows it would be kinder to shoot it than let it suffer.

Her father had always said that when a hare, a fox or even a dog had been caught in a gin trap, which was a particularly cruel trap, there was no chance of saving their legs, which would have been broken and the flesh lacerated and the quicker they died the better.

Arletta hated the idea of killing anything, but she knew that it was far kinder than to let the animal continue to screech in agony.

She therefore put her hand under the pillow and drew out the little Russian revolver and slipped it into the pocket of her negligée.

As she pulled the furniture away from the door, she knew that if she carried one of the candles, the draughts that blew through parts of the Château might cause it to be blown out, so she picked up the oil lamp.

She went slowly down the twisting stairs, lighting her way with the lamp and, when she reached the corridor, it was easy to see her way by the candles in their silver sconces.

There was nobody about and, having reached the ground floor, she continued down a narrow staircase, which she reckoned, although she had not been there before, led to the dungeons.

She had taken only a few steps when a voice behind her asked,

"What are you doing? Where are you going?"

She was startled so that the oil in the lamp swung a little precariously before she turned round.

It was the Duc who stood above her at the entrance to the stairway and, because for the moment she could not speak, he asked again,

"What are you doing at this time of night and why are you going down to the dungeons?"

He was still wearing the evening clothes that he had worn at dinner and Arletta was immediately conscious that she was wearing a negligée and her fair hair was falling over her shoulders as he had seen it once before.

As she looked up at the Duc, she saw that the expression on his face was not exactly one of anger, but, she thought, of suspicion.

It flashed through her mind that he thought she was meeting somebody surreptitiously, perhaps the Comte, in the dungeons.

Quickly, because she was embarrassed, she answered him,

"There is an animal caught in a trap, *monsieur*, and it is screaming in pain. It woke me up."

"An animal?" the Duc repeated.

"Yes, *monsieur*, it is directly below my window in the tower."

"And you say you cannot sleep?"

"I was asleep, but I realised that I could not ignore it when it was in such agony."

Arletta felt that she was explaining herself badly and thought for a moment that he did not believe her.

Then he said,

"If that is so, we must certainly do something about it. Let me take the lamp from you."

He came down the stairs, which were wider than those at the side of the tower.

He took the lamp from her hand and then went ahead, holding it high so that it lit the way.

Down, down they went and, as Arletta followed the Duc below ground, she felt that he must think her very foolish.

When the stairs came to an end and they were in a circular chamber having the same dimensions as the tower above, she was aware of heavy iron doors that must be the entrance to the dungeons.

It was then, almost to her relief, that she heard faintly the screams that had awakened her and knew that the Duc must hear them too.

He was standing in the centre of the chamber waiting for her to follow him down the last few steps.

He turned his head towards the sound that Arletta had spoken about and said,

"It obviously comes from here."

He opened the door of one of the dungeons and now the noise as it echoed round the stone walls seemed almost deafening.

The dungeon was very small and was just high enough for a man to stand upright in and there was a window just below the stone ceiling, which was heavily barred with only an inch between each of the bars.

Arletta could see that even in the daytime the window was too small to let in very much light, but this was where the sound was coming from.

Holding the lamp as high as he could, the Duc moved to the window and, as Arletta followed him, she saw that tied to one of the iron bars was an animal struggling to free itself and screaming as it did so.

For a moment it was just something dark, which made it difficult to determine what it could be.

Then, as the Duc shone the light on it, Arletta saw that it was a small cat with black and white fur.

It was little more than a kitten, but old enough to make an almost deafening noise and the Duc looked at it for a long moment before he asked her,

"Hold the lamp for me while I release it."

"It will fall into the river," Arletta said quickly.

"I think it will save itself if it is freed," he replied.

She took the lamp from him and he struggled to undo the knot of the cord that fastened the cat's leg to the iron bar.

Because it would have been impossible to have squeezed the cat through the bars, Arletta knew that two people must have been involved in torturing the wretched animal in such a hideous manner.

She could not see the Duc's face because he had his back to her, but she realised perceptively that he was very angry.

'It must have been somebody in the Château who has done this,' she surmised.

She wondered if the Duc would find out who the culprit was and what punishment he would inflict upon him.

It seemed to take a long time before he finally pulled the string into the dungeon and as he did so the cat gave a shrill scream and it fell down into the river or against the foundation stones of the Château.

But whichever it was, after it had vanished there was silence and then the Duc turned towards Arletta.

She saw that he was frowning and she asked,

"Who could have done anything so cruel?"

"That is what I would like to know," the Duc said ominously.

"I will tell you who it was," a voice came from the doorway.

They both turned round and as they did so the Duc took the lamp from Arletta as if he wanted to see who had spoken.

To her astonishment it was Comte Jacques.

"You know who tortured this wretched animal?" the Duc demanded harshly.

"I did," the Comte volunteered. "It was a 'sprat to catch a mackerel'. But what a surprise! My bait, a very effective one, has captured not one fish but two!"

"I don't know what you are talking about," the Duc snapped, "but you can tell me when we get out of here."

"That is where you are mistaken, my dear cousin," the Comte replied. "You are not leaving here, not for a moment or two. I think you will understand what I mean when I tell you that I have my hand on the lever of the trapdoor."

The Duc stiffened and Arletta felt as if her heart had suddenly stopped beating.

She saw now that, exactly as David had described it, just inside the dungeon there was a lever and the Comte's right hand was resting on it as he himself was standing in the round chamber at the door of the dungeon.

He had only to exert a little pressure on it and the floor would open beneath them and they would fall down into the cage at the bottom of the river where they would drown.

It all flashed through her mind.

At the same time she thought that she must be dreaming and what was happening could not be true.

"What are you talking about, Jacques?" the Duc asked again.

Now he was speaking quietly and deliberately slowly, slightly drawling his words.

"I think you understand, my dear cousin or at least you should by now," the Comte asserted, "that I have no intention of allowing you to be involved with a young woman, however attractive and however fascinating."

"I have no idea what you are saying to me," the Duc reacted sternly, "and I suggest we leave this very unpleasant, cold damp place and talk sensibly outside."

"I enticed Mademoiselle here," Comte Jacques carried on, "because, when I saw you looking at her in a way I considered dangerous to my future, I knew if she disappeared without any trace, as I planned, who would be blamed!"

"Of course," the Duc agreed, "there would be no doubt about that."

The Comte laughed and Arletta felt that there was a distinctly mad note in his merriment.

"No one had any idea, did they, Cousin Etienne," he jeered, "that it was I who pushed your wife over the battlements! You left her crying and it was easy, almost too easy, to make sure that she did not produce the son who would have disinherited me."

As he spoke, Arletta started and she began to understand now what this was all about.

"As you say," the Duc said slowly, "you were very clever and no one suspected you, Jacques."

"I made sure of that," he boasted.

"I suppose," the Duc said and now his voice was cynical, as it had been when Arletta first arrived at the Château, "you also killed Madeleine Monsarrat."

"Of course!" the Comte replied. "It was easy, because she was always drinking coffee, to put an overdose of laudanum into her cup. Poor Cousin Etienne, you really have been very unjustly accused."

"I am only surprised that you have left *me* alone for so long!" the Duc remarked.

"I was just a little worried in case your sudden disappearance might focus on the fact that I am the next Duc," the Comte retorted. "But now you and the delectable English teacher will disappear and, of course, I shall spread the rumour that you have run away together. There will be no other possible explanation."

Arletta gave a cry.

"How can you think of – anything so diabolical – so wicked?"

As if for the first time she drew his attention, the Comte parried,

"You have no one to blame but yourself! I tried to take you away from the Duc, if you remember, by inviting you to come with me to Paris."

"I cannot really believe you ever thought I would consider – such an idea," Arletta said angrily.

"Why not?" the Comte asked. "We would have enjoyed ourselves together, I would have made sure of that and I should not have been afraid of my cousin becoming infatuated with you, as he was with the Comtesse."

"But you cannot – mean to do anything so – terrible as to – kill us!"

Arletta tried to speak pleadingly, but her voice trembled and she knew how frightened she was.

"I am told that drowning is quite a pleasant death," the Comte answered, "and, although I shall be sorry to lose the company of my delightful and charming cousin, I shall make up for his loss by being a most exemplary and dashing Duc."

He looked down at Arletta as he spoke and she reckoned that it was only a question of seconds before he pulled the lever.

"Now, listen, Jacques," the Duc said harshly, "I have something to suggest to you."

"What is it?"

"Drown me if you wish to, but spare Mademoiselle's life. She has nothing to do with our quarrels or the succession of the Ducs of Sauterre. She is English. Let her go back to her own country and forget that she has ever been involved in anything quite so unsavoury."

The Comte laughed and it was a very unpleasant sound.

"A heroic suggestion!" he sneered. "But I am not quite so foolish, my dear cousin, as to let a woman free who would talk. And what woman would not talk in such circumstances?"

He laughed again and went on,

"There is nothing you can do, *nothing*! I have beaten you, as I always wanted to, and now I have won!"

As he spoke the word '*won*', it brought back to Arletta the witch's words that she was a winner and also that she was the only person who could save herself.

She thrust her right hand into the pocket of her negligée and grasped the butt of the little jewelled revolver.

"Goodbye, Cousin Etienne!" the Comte was crowing triumphantly. "I am sorry there is no time for you to say your – prayers."

Before he could finish the last word, Arletta drew out the revolver and shot straight at him.

The explosion seemed to echo deafeningly around the small chamber and she felt almost as if it cracked her eardrums.

Then, as the Comte took his hand from the lever to clutch at his shoulder where the bullet had struck him, the Duc stepped forward.

Regardless of the fact that he held the oil lamp in his left hand, he hit the Comte with the clenched fist of his right hand on the point of the chin.

With a groan he staggered back against the stone wall unconscious and then he slid slowly down from it to the floor.

As he did so, his evening coat flew open and Arletta saw the crimson blood already staining his white shirt.

The Duc turned back to hold out his hand to Arletta.

As she took it, feeling as if it was a lifeline, he pulled her out of the dungeon and into the chamber outside.

It was then that the horror of what had happened swept over her and she held onto the Duc, hiding her face against his shoulder.

He put the oil lamp down on the protruding part of a buttress and then he put both his arms around her.

"It's all right," he said gently, "it's all right and you have saved us both."

"D-did I – k-kill him?"

It was difficult to speak the words because her teeth were chattering.

"No, he is alive," the Duc replied, "but I will deal with him later."

Still with one arm round her he drew her back to the door that they had entered the chamber through and shut and bolted it, leaving the Comte inside.

Then he said,

"I have to carry the lamp. Do you think you can walk up the stairs?"

"I am – all – right."

The Duc did not take his arm from her, but, picking up the lamp to light their way, they moved slowly side by side up the stairs until they reached the corridor at the top.

There was a table in the passage just beside the entrance to the stairway and the Duc put the lamp down on it.

Then, aware that Arletta was almost fainting, he picked her up in his arms.

She wanted to protest that she could manage to walk, but the words would not come and instead she hid her face against his shoulder and, as she did so, she started to weep.

As the Duc carried her back along the passage and up a few stairs, she did not look or even wonder where they were going.

She merely went on crying against him.

Only when he stopped walking and put her feet down on the ground, still keeping his arms around her, did she raise her head.

"It's all right, *ma chérie*," he breathed very quietly. "We are both alive and I promise you that this will never happen again."

The way he spoke, the deepness in his voice and the endearment seemed to seep through the sense of shock that Arletta was feeling and check her tears.

She raised her face, looking up at him in bewilderment and, as she did so, his arms tightened and he drew her closer.

He did not speak, but she had the strange feeling that she could feel his heart beating against hers.

Then his lips came down on her lips.

CHAPTER SEVEN

For a moment all Arletta could feel was the hardness of his lips against hers.

Then, as he held her closer still and felt her mouth soft and trembling, his kiss became more insistent and more demanding.

Because she had never before been kissed, Arletta had no idea that it would mean sensations rising within her that were different from anything that she could have known or felt possible.

And yet it was all the rapture of her dreams as well as all the beauty of her imagination enveloping everything that she saw and felt.

The Duc kissed her until she felt as if she had died and in some amazing way was in Heaven.

It seemed impossible that she could be alive and on earth and feel at the same time that she was part of the music of the spheres with angels singing around her.

When she thought that it was impossible to feel any more, while her body quivered with the rapture that was so inexpressible and so wonderful that she could only pray that it would never stop, the Duc raised his head.

He looked down at her, at her eyes wet with tears and yet shining with a radiance that seemed to light up the schoolroom where he had carried her.

For a moment they just looked at each other, but, when he would have kissed her again, Arletta gave an inarticulate little murmur and hid her face against his neck.

He held her close against him, his lips on her hair and then said in a voice that sounded deep and unsteady,

"You must go to bed, my precious, and I must deal with that devil below who intended us to die tonight."

"How – could he have tried to do such – terrible things to – you?" Arletta whispered.

Her words, because of the depth of her feeling, were almost inarticulate, but the Duc heard her and asked,

"You are thinking of me?"

"I-I had to – save you."

"As you did, most effectively."

He was aware, as she was speaking to him, that she swayed and he picked her up in his arms and carried her from the schoolroom onto the twisting staircase.

There was just room for him to take her up past the rooms where the children slept and into her own bedroom.

Although she had taken the oil lamp with her that was beside her bed when she went to the dungeons, she had left two candles alight on either side of the mirror on her dressing table.

The Duc carried her to the bed and laid her down very gently.

As he smiled at her, she put her hands up to him and said with a touch of fear returning to her voice,

"P-please – don't – leave me."

"I must," he answered, "but you will be all right."

"Will you – come back and – tell me if the Comte is dead?" Arletta faltered.

Then with a little cry she added,

"If he – d-dies – will I have to – stand trial?"

The Duc sat down on the bed and took her hands in his.

"There will be no trial. Jacques is not dead, which in some ways is a pity. I will deal with him and try to put right all the evil he has perpetuated."

There was a hard note in his voice as he spoke and Arletta held onto him as she stammered,

"You are – quite certain if you – go back to him now – that he will not – manage in some way to – k-kill you?"

"You would mind if he did?" the Duc enquired.

She gazed at him for a moment not comprehending what he was saying.

Then, as she understood, the colour crept up her face and the Duc thought that it was the most beautiful thing he had ever seen.

"There is no need to answer that question, *ma belle*," he said. "You love me as I love you and we will talk about it later."

He bent forward and she thought that he would kiss her lips, but instead he kissed her forehead.

"Get into bed and rest," he went on. "I may be some time, but I promise I will come back to tell you what has happened."

He kissed her hair and then, as she watched him, her eyes seeming to fill the whole of her face, he left the bedroom, shutting the door behind him.

She listened until she could no longer hear his footsteps going down the stairs.

Then she closed her eyes as if she could not believe that she had not been dreaming the weird and terrible things that had happened.

At the same time what she remembered more vividly than anything else was the feel of the Duc's wondrous lips on hers.

*

A long time later, as the first faint glow of the dawn was breaking in the sky, the Duc knocked gently on the door and then came into Arletta's bedroom.

She was lying back against the pillows, her long fair hair falling over her shoulders.

She had been unable to sleep and instead was praying fervently that now that the Comte had been unmasked and his wicked plotting against the Duc exposed, there would no longer be the whispering in the Château that had been so prevalent since she had arrived.

She understood now why it had affected everybody who was living there including the two children.

It had poisoned the atmosphere and prevented it from being, as she so wanted, a Château of happiness and love.

'Now the Duc can be happy and look happy,' she told herself.

Then, as if a knife pierced her heart, she thought that there would be no reason, now that she had saved him, why he would want her after she had finished teaching David English.

There would be women as beautiful as the Marquise, who would love him even though they were married.

There would be other women like the Comtesse, whom the Comte had killed, whom he would love and one of them would make him a suitable wife.

'He kissed me just in gratitude,' she told herself.

While to her it had been the most wonderful thing that had ever happened, to him she was just another woman he had kissed in a long line of beauties.

'I *love* – him,' she admitted to herself at last and knew that it was inevitable when he was so handsome and so magnificent.

But, because he had been cynical and unhappy, it had in a way been a challenge that she could not resist.

She felt that she had wanted to help him or at least find out about him, perhaps from the first moment that she had seen him, staring at her in amazement as she had danced under the chandeliers in the Château ballroom.

Looking back, she had first been intrigued by what Jane had told her about him and then by the way that the Duchesse had accused her of trying to 'catch' him and, of course, by all the tales that everybody in the Château and the children had told her.

'Now the darkness and shadows that spoiled everything have been lifted,' she pondered. 'I have saved his life and there is nothing more I can do for him.'

She tried to think about it logically and calmly, yet she could only remember his arms around her and the way his lips had sent electric thrills through her whole body.

She felt again the ecstasy he had given her and the rapture that was part of her prayers. She knew that it was not only something she could never forget but that she would never find it with any other man.

It was a white and worried little face that Arletta turned towards the Duc as he came towards her bed, looking, she thought, so magnificent in his evening clothes and so elegant that he might have come straight from a Royal dinner party.

There was a smile on his lips and she could see by the light of the candles that he looked happy and, she believed, younger.

"You are still awake?" he asked. "I hoped you would sleep."

He reached her side and stood looking down at her and, impulsively because she could not prevent herself, she held out both her arms.

"You are – safe! He – did not – hurt you?"

The Duc smiled and sat down on the bed, taking her hands in his.

He kissed them both and then turned them over to kiss first one palm and then the other.

It was a gesture that had never happened to Arletta before and she felt a thrill sweep through her that was like a streak of lightning.

As the Duc felt not only her fingers but her whole body quiver, he said,

"My precious, I have so many things to tell you, far more important than what has just happened."

"I-I have to – know," she stuttered

He gave a sigh and then, holding both her hands in his, he started,

"I took Byien and my Major Domo with me down to the dungeons where you and I left Jacques."

"He is – alive?"

"Very much alive," the Duc answered, "and swearing and cursing in a manner that has made me realise, as I should have done before, that his brain is unhinged."

"I thought he – must be – mad!"

"That is the kindest thing we can say about him."

"What have you – done with – him?"

"I have taken him to the doctor who looks after everybody in the Château. He has a small hospital, a very small one, where the bullet that lodged in his shoulder when you shot him will be extracted. However, I have made sure that he will not escape from there and tomorrow I will deal with his future."

"There will – not be a – trial?"

Arletta's voice trembled with anxiety.

"Because I cannot have you involved in this and also because, as you will understand, I wish to have no scandal surrounding my family and so Jacques will be treated far better than he deserves."

"W-what do you – mean?"

"I am planning to have him sent to an estate I own in French Colonial Africa. There he will stay working on a farm until he dies. If he returns to France, he will be arrested."

The Duc's voice was firm, but not hard and Arletta queried,

"I think you – are being – too kind."

"As I have already said, far kinder than he deserves," the Duc declared, "and very much kinder than the way he treated us."

"You had no notion that he was – obsessed with the idea – of taking – your place?"

"I did not realise that Jacques had killed my wife although I knew that it was he who had spread the rumour that I had killed her because we quarrelled."

He then paused and, because she hated to think how much he had suffered from the whispering campaign against him, Arletta's fingers tightened on his.

"I guessed, however, that it was what had happened," the Duc continued, "when my friend, Madeleine Montsarrat, died of an overdose of laudanum."

He paused and in a very small voice Arletta asked,

"Were you – very much in love with – her?"

"I loved her as much as I was capable of loving anyone at that moment," the Duc admitted, "and I felt that she would make me a very suitable wife and give me the children I wanted."

Again it seemed to Arletta that a knife pierced her heart. She did not speak and the Duc went on.

"Then, when I became aware that it was Jacques who was making me hated and feared, not only by everybody in the Château and on my estate but in the world outside, I could not think of a way to stop him."

"Did you – speak to him – about it?" Arletta asked.

"What would have been the point? He would only have denied being the originator of such tales. I suppose too I was proud, too proud to argue and plead with a man I utterly despised."

"I can – understand."

She thought that it was the Duc's pride that had made his tongue so sarcastic and him look so cynical because he would not admit, even to himself, that he was being manipulated by his disreputable cousin.

"Then you came," the Duc said in a low voice, "and I was really frightened."

"Frightened?"

It was a word that Arletta would never have imagined him using.

He smiled before he answered very gently.

"I fell in love with you, my alluring, fascinating little teacher, when I saw you dancing under the chandeliers in the ballroom and wearing very little to hide your exquisite figure."

Arletta blushed, but was too shy to look directly at the Duc as she asked,

"Were you – very shocked?"

"I was intrigued. At the same time I knew indisputably that I had found what I have been seeking all my life."

"How could you have – known that?"

"You are not the only person, my lovely one, who is perceptive."

"I-I knew you were – but not – me."

"I am very very perceptive about you," the Duc stated firmly. "But I realised that Jacques was watching us and, although I could hardly believe that he would destroy you as he had already destroyed two other women in my life, I was desperately afraid."

He gave a deep sigh before he carried on.

"I blame myself for not, as I ought to have done, sending you back to England as being a very unsuitable Governess."

Arletta gave a little cry.

"I was so afraid that you – might after you had seen – me in the ballroom. But I wanted to – stay here. I desperately wanted to – stay."

"So you stayed," the Duc said, "but it might, if you had not saved us both, been a tragedy that nobody would ever have known the true explanation about."

The way he spoke made Arletta say,

"We are safe, but promise me you will see that we remain so and he cannot – escape to – somehow try – again."

"I swear to you that will never happen and now, my darling, I am free to ask you if you will be my wife."

Arletta stared at him.

Then she said,

"Did you say – are you really asking me to – *marry* you?"

"I love you, as I have never loved anybody before," the Duc asserted, "and I think you love me."

"It – cannot be – true!"

"It *is* true!" he insisted. "And, as I do *not* intend to risk losing you as I might have done tonight, I am determined to marry you immediately. Then I will be able to look after you a great deal better than I have done up to now."

There was a dazzling light in Arletta's eyes.

At the same time, because it was impossible for her to comprehend entirely what the Duc was saying to her, she faltered,

"You cannot – it is not right for you – and you don't even – know who – I am."

The Duc chuckled and it was a very happy sound.

"I know that you are somebody I love and who is everything I want in a woman and who, although you may not realise it, is already part of my heart and my soul, if indeed I have one!"

"B-but – I am not – Jane – Turner!"

"I am well aware of that."

"You are? But – how?"

"Because, my beautiful one, Lady Langley, when she persuaded me to engage a Governess for David, told me,

"'If you are worried that Miss Turner will disrupt your household in any way, let me assure you that she is a very sensible young woman of twenty-eight and rather plain, poor thing, so I am afraid that no man will ever look at her, but she is very competent and kind'."

The Duc smiled again as he remarked,

"Only the last two adjectives apply to you."

"So you – guessed from the – beginning that I was not – Jane!"

"To begin with by no stretch of the imagination could you be twenty-eight," the Duc said. "How old are you?"

"I am twenty."

"And your name?"

"Is Arletta. That is true. It slipped out by mistake."

"I guessed that too," he said, "and, although it makes no difference to me who you are, I shall have to know the rest of your name before I fill in the forms that are compulsory in a French marriage."

"My name is – Cherrington-Weir," Arletta informed him shyly. "My father, who died only a few weeks ago, was the sixth Earl of Weir."

She did not wait for the Duc to comment, but went on,

"What I have longed to tell you, because I felt that you would be interested, was that my mother's mother was the Comtesse de Falaise, who came from Normandy, and I was called after her."

She looked at the Duc apprehensively as she spoke in case she had said anything wrong.

Then he exclaimed,

"I cannot believe it! The Falaises are directly related to my family and we are therefore, my darling, of the same blood as well as being united in every other way."

Arletta gave a cry of delight.

"I am glad, so very very glad! I think *Grandmère*, whom I adored, would be pleased too."

"So will my grandmother."

"I am sure if I really had been Jane Turner," Arletta replied, "she would have been shocked at her grandson making a marriage that could only be described as a *mésalliance*. She made it quite plain that she suspected that I had come here specifically to 'catch' you!"

"That is exactly what you have done!" the Duc said. "Actually, *Grandmère* will be so grateful that you have saved my life that I think anything else about you would have paled into insignificance. But now she will, my precious precious, not that it matters, approve of you wholeheartedly."

"Can I – really – marry you?"

"I have every intention that you shall," the Duc insisted, "and, although I have a great deal to teach you, my adorable little twenty-year-old Teacher, you have so much to teach me."

She looked surprised and he explained.

"I have already had a few lectures from you and now it is up to you to fill the Château with love and happiness and make certain that it is as beautiful inside as it is out."

Arletta gave a deep sigh before she said,

"Can you – really mean to marry me when you – hate the English so ferociously?"

She was too shy to look at him as she asked the question and she was suddenly anxious as he took his hand away from hers.

Then he said,

"I expected you to ask me that question and there is a lot of explaining to do as to why I hated your countrymen until you came and changed everything. Will you, however, answer one question that I am going to put to you?"

"Yes, of course," Arletta nodded.

"Will you tell me," the Duc asked, "that you are aware, as I am, that nothing really matters except the love we know exists between us and that it is different from anything else in this whole wide world?"

Arletta was about to speak, but he went on.

"Nationality, family, social importance, titles, money, can any of them compare with what you felt just now when I kissed you and what for me was an emotional experience that I have never had in all of my life?"

"Is that – really true?"

"I think you know that what I am saying is the truth," the Duc said solemnly. "I adore you, Arletta, and I worship you because you are everything a woman should be and I thought I would never ever find you."

He spoke so solemnly with every word vibrating in her heart and Arletta put up her arms and pulled his head down to hers.

She had the feeling as she did so that he had deliberately not kissed her when he came to her bedroom because he had thought that it might make her shy or even shocked.

Now she pulled him close to her and his lips were on hers.

Once again there was the rapture, the wonder and the ecstasy and, as he carried her into the sky, they were part of God.

Then, when she wanted him to kiss her and go on kissing her, he deliberately moved and said,

"You are not to tempt me, *ma belle*, until we are married. Then I can teach you about love without being afraid of frightening you or making you feel that you are doing something that your mother and your grandmother would think was wrong."

The way he spoke made her remember the Comte and Arletta sighed,

"You are – looking after – me and – protecting me."

"That is exactly what I intend to do and now, my darling, I am going to tell you why I hated the English. But before I do so, there is one thing I want to say."

"What is – it?" Arletta asked a little nervously.

They were talking, as they always had, in French, and now the Duc said quietly,

"*Je t'aime*! I cannot say it too often and I will also say it in your language. *I love you*!"

He spoke in English and Arletta stared at him in amazement.

"You speak English?"

"Almost as well as you speak French."

"Is that – true? I cannot – believe it!"

"Then let me explain. The reason why I loathed the English was that my mother died when I was ten and two years later my father married an Englishwoman."

~171~

Arletta gave a little gasp.

"An – Englishwoman!"

"I should have said rather that *she* married *him*!" the Duc went on in a hard voice. "He was a sick man, broken in body and spirit because he had lost the wife he loved and she tricked him into becoming his wife."

"I am – sorry," Arletta sympathised, sensing how much it had obviously hurt him.

"She wanted," the Duc went on, "not only to be the Duchesse de Sauterre but also to produce the next Duc, thus cutting me out. Because she was unable to do so, owing to my father's bad health, she made my life a living Hell. She tortured me as only a small, rather oversensitive boy can be tortured with a mental cruelty that made me loathe her. In fact she was hated by everyone in the Château, including my grandmother."

"Why did nobody tell me – this?" Arletta asked.

"When I was eighteen, just before my father died and I inherited the title, my stepmother had a fatal riding accident," the Duc replied. "As her death was a relief and a deliverance, it was agreed that her name would never be mentioned again by those who had known her and her diabolical treatment of me."

"I am sorry – so desperately sorry."

"You can therefore understand," the Duc carried on, "that, when my sister married an Englishman, I opposed it with every means in my power, thinking that we all might have to suffer again from the cruelty and spite of someone English."

His lips twisted in a faint smile as he resumed,

"Actually Gerald was a very quiet unassuming character, but my stepmother's treatment of me had gone too deep for me to forget or forgive."

"Now I can – understand," Arletta murmured.

"I knew you would and I confess that I was wrong, completely and absolutely wrong, to try to turn David against his own countrymen and prevent him from going to his father's school."

Because he was naturally so proud, Arletta realised that this admission was a tremendous effort and so she said very gently,

"You have made amends for all that. Can I really help you to – forget what you have – suffered?"

She looked at him anxiously as she went on,

"Suppose there is some – dark spot in our love – that I cannot – change and which – as the years go by – makes you – hate me?"

The Duc laughed.

"Do you really think, my darling, that I could possibly hate you?" he asked in English. "I have already told you that I adore and worship you and I know that you will bring me everything that is best in England, just as I will try to give you everything that is the very best in France."

"That is what I – want to – think," Arletta said, "and I will do – everything I can to make you – happy."

"All you have to do is to love me," the Duc asserted solemnly. "It is what I have missed since my mother died and what I need desperately for myself and then one day for my children."

"I will give it to you – I swear I will give it to you!" Arletta cried.

Once again she held out her arms and the Duc kissed her.

She thought as he did so that there was something Holy and reverent in his kiss that had not been there before.

Then, when he raised his head, there was no longer any need for the light from the candles for the first rays of the sun were coming in through the East window, illuminating the whole room with a golden light.

"Now I am going to leave you," he said, "and you are to go to sleep. Dream of me and forget all the horrors that have happened, because they are of no consequence now."

"You will still be here in – the morning?" Arletta asked. "You will not vanish and I will find this has – all been a – wonderful – wonderful dream?"

"I will be here not only tomorrow and the day after but for the rest of our lives together."

He kissed her hand and then he rose, blew out the candles and walked towards the door.

"Good night, my perfect and most beloved wife-to-be," he pronounced in English. "I love you!"

Then he was gone and Arletta suddenly felt tears of happiness running down her cheeks.

*

The little Church outside the great gates of the Château was decorated with white lilies.

Apart from the bride and the bridegroom and Monsieur Byien, who was the Duc's best man, there was nobody else in the Church.

The village Priest officiated with two Servers and Arletta felt that the empty aisles were filled with the spirits of those who had lived in the Château for so many generations and had worshipped there.

They had left behind them their prayers and faith that she had been so vividly conscious of the first time she had prayed in the old Church.

She had asked the Duc to see that all the candles were lit before the statue of Joan of Arc and, when he looked surprised, she had told him,

"I lit one the first time I came here and I prayed that somehow the shadows over the Château would go away and I think too in my heart that I prayed for you."

"Then we must certainly be grateful to the Saint," the Duc smiled.

Because the Duc was of such local importance, the Mayor had come from the nearest town to the Château earlier in the morning and had married them according to French law.

After he had left, the Duc had walked with Arletta across the great courtyard and into the Church.

He had announced, because Arletta was in mourning, that there would be no guests at the Wedding.

But he had added that the staff from the Château and everybody in the village would be entertained later in one of the huge rooms that were used for such occasions.

And, as the Church was so small, the bride and bridegroom would be married quietly and alone.

It was a slightly surprising arrangement, but the villagers would not think of disobeying the Duc and were appeased at being excluded from the Ceremony by the fact that

David and Pauline waited just outside the door to shower them with rose petals.

As soon as they realised what the children were about to do, the villagers picked the petals from every flower in their gardens.

When Arletta and the Duc came out through the great arched door, they were enveloped with clouds of petals so that their walk from the Church back to the Château was literally, Arletta pointed out with a smile, 'a path of roses'.

"This is what our life together will be," the Duc smiled.

The way he spoke and the love in his eyes made her feel as if she was still moving in the Fairyland that she had felt she inhabited ever since she awoke.

The morning after the drama in the dungeon she had slept, as she had not expected to, until luncheontime.

It was the housekeeper who had brought her a meal on a tray at one o'clock saying,

"Monsieur le Duc's explicit orders, *m'mselle*, and you're to stay in bed until you're really rested."

"But – it is so late," Arletta protested. "I had no idea I could sleep for so long."

"It's certainly not surprisin', *m'mselle*," the housekeeper told her in a repressed tone, "seein' all you've been through. But you must be sensible and realise it's been a real shock to the system."

Arletta knew then that the whole household of the Château would be aware of exactly what had happened.

It was one of the reasons why the Duc wished her to stay quietly in her room so that she would not have to be involved in the explanations that would have be made or in answering innumerable questions if she was downstairs.

She did as he wished and only when he suggested that, when she was dressed, he would like to see her at five o'clock did she eagerly go down to his study where he was waiting for her.

As she entered the room, she stood for a moment just inside the door.

Then, as he held out his arms, she ran towards him, feeling that there was really no need for her to hear what had happened.

They were one and she loved him so overwhelmingly that nothing else mattered.

They sat and talked for a long time.

And then he suggested,

"I am going to send you back to bed, my darling. You have been through an experience that would leave most women prostrate and I have so much to arrange that it is impossible to complete them all if you are beside me."

"You don't – want me?" Arletta asked provocatively.

"I will answer that question tomorrow after we are married," he replied.

"Tomorrow?"

"I told you that I was not going to wait any longer. You are mine, Arletta, and only when you are my wife will I feel no longer afraid of losing you."

She realised as he spoke that just as she had been horrified by the terror that the Comte had inflicted on them in the dungeon, so for the Duc, because he loved her, it had been a ghastly experience to think that he could not protect her as he wished to do.

She remembered how he had begged the Comte to spare her life and she felt that no man could be more wonderful or more loving.

She was prepared to allow him to know what was best for them both without argument.

In fact she thought with a little smile as she went back to her bedroom as he had virtually commanded her to do that he would always be her Master.

It would be impossible to fight against him even though she might coax him with love into doing what she wanted.

She therefore went to bed, her whole being vibrating from the wonder of his kisses and feeling that her head was in the clouds because of the plans that he was making for them both.

"We will be married tomorrow," the Duc had said, "and on the following day we will leave for my Villa in the South of France, where we shall be alone with nobody to disturb us, and I will tell you of my love for you in great detail."

"You – know that is – what I want," Arletta said with a little quiver of excitement in her voice. "At the same time – we must not forget David."

The Duc smiled.

"I thought that was something you would say and I have not forgotten David. I have already arranged for an Englishman who is studying French at the University of Limoges to come here in our absence and stay until we return, or perhaps longer, if you approve of him."

As Arletta gave a cry of delight, the Duc added,

"Incidentally he is very keen on cricket and I suggested to him that he form a team from amongst the footmen and the other young men on the estate."

Arletta clasped her hands together.

"How can you be so – wonderful as to think of – everything?"

"I think of you," the Duc replied and she knew that it was the truth.

*

When Arletta awoke very early on her Wedding morning, she found that he had thought of her in more ways than one.

The housekeeper brought a Wedding gown to the room that had been worn by the Duc's mother on her Wedding Day and which was only a trifle too large for her in the waist.

Otherwise it fitted her very well.

Of white satin with a very full skirt, the top was a lace bertha off the shoulder, which was embroidered all over with tiny diamanté and pearls.

It was so lovely that Arletta could hardly believe when she saw herself in the mirror that it had not been specially designed for her.

With the exquisite Brussels lace veil, which the de Sauterres had worn for generations, and a diamond tiara, she looked like the Fairy Princess she had visualised herself as being when she had first come to the Château.

When she came down from the tower for the last time, since tonight she would be in the State bedroom, where the Duchesse de Sauterre had slept through the ages, there was a bouquet of white orchids for her to carry.

The Duc was waiting for her, attired, as was the custom for Frenchmen, in full evening dress.

He looked so magnificent with a ribbon across his white shirt and a number of jewelled Orders on his coat that Arletta could only gasp in admiration.

Then, as he kissed her hand, he said,

"You look as I wanted you to look. As my bride and as the Saint who lives in a shrine in my heart."

After their Wedding they went up to see the Duchesse and, as if she wanted to celebrate the occasion, she was festooned in even more jewellery than Arletta had seen her wear before.

She kissed the old lady and so did the Duc and the Duchesse then said,

"You see? I was right! I knew you had come here to ensnare my grandson!"

"As I am very willing to be," the Duc grinned.

The Duchesse chuckled and then she addressed Arletta,

"I have not only to thank you, my dear, for saving my grandson's life but also for saving me from having to see his despicable cousin take his place as the new Duc!"

"You are not to speak of it," the Duc interposed.

"I have not yet finished, Etienne," the Duchesse said firmly. "I only wanted to tell Arletta that she is the best and most beautiful woman who has ever come to the Château and that we all love her, every one of us!"

Because she was so moved, Arletta felt the tears come into her eyes.

Then, when the Duchesse had drunk their health in champagne and they had kissed her again, they left the room.

The old maid was waiting outside.

"You've made Madame ever so happy, *monsieur*," she said to the Duc. "I've never known her so thrilled or so delighted as she is today."

"That is what I am feeling myself," the Duc admitted as he and Arletta went downstairs.

There was one more party to attend, which was the luncheon arranged for the staff, the tenants and the labourers on the estate.

The huge room, which Arletta learnt had once been where revels had taken place in Medieval times, was decorated with flowers and bunting.

There were long trestle tables groaning with food, although how it had been organised so quickly she could not imagine until she learned that the chefs had been working literally all night.

There was home-brewed cider as well as wine for everybody who wanted it and David was particularly excited because the Duc had told him that in his absence he was to play host.

He sat at the head of one of the long trestle tables and Pauline at the other and Arletta knew that it was impossible for the two children to be more thrilled by the responsibilities that the Duc had given them.

The Duc made a speech thanking everybody for their congratulations and good wishes and saying that a new era of happiness had begun at the Château and it was up to them to make certain that everybody forgot the unhappiness of the last few years.

As he spoke, Arletta swore in her heart that she would make up for all that everyone else had suffered.

They left the party to go back alone to their own luncheon, which was arranged in one of the smaller rooms that Arletta had not seen before.

What she ate and drank she had no idea, because, although while the servants were in the room, they talked of ordinary things, the Duc's eyes were telling her of his great love.

It was impossible to think of anything but the sensations he aroused in her.

When at last they were alone, she thought that he would take her into the study.

Instead they walked up the grand staircase towards the State rooms and now she thought that he would perhaps take her to the ballroom where he had watched her dancing alone and claimed that it was there he had fallen in love with her.

Instead he went on down the long corridor to where at the end was his own bedroom, the most important in the whole house.

Next to it was the room that the housekeeper had told Arletta she would occupy when she left the tower bedroom.

David had not shown her these rooms on her tour of the house because the shutters were closed in the Duchesse's room and he was too nervous to take her into his uncle's.

Now Arletta found that the rooms were more beautiful than anything she could imagine in her dreams.

What was more, her room was decorated with white flowers, which, in contrast to the pale blue brocade walls, made a perfect background for the colourful Fragonard pictures, which were appropriately of lovers and cupids.

There was a huge canopied bed carved with gilded cupids under a ceiling depicting Venus rising from the foam.

"I shall not feel – real in such a beautiful room," Arletta said in an awe-stricken little voice.

"Come and look at mine," the Duc suggested.

He opened a communicating door and she found that his room was even larger than hers.

It was decorated in almost the same manner, but was more masculine. The bed was hung with curtains of red velvet with the de Sauterre crest over a carved and gilt headboard.

What was surprising, she thought, was that the flowers that decorated his room as well as hers were white orchids and lilies.

As she looked round, she realised that the Duc had closed the door and was now closer to her. And she thought that he was about to kiss her.

Instead he lifted the tiara from her head and put it on top of a chest.

Then he took off her lace veil and threw it over a chair.

She waited, accepting that he wanted to do things his own way, but longing for him to kiss her. She felt as if her whole body was pulsating with a heavenly rapture while she waited for him to do so.

Instead he drew the hairpins from her hair and it fell over her shoulders in soft waves.

"Now you look as you did the first time I saw you," he said in a deep voice, "except, my darling, that you have on far more clothes than you had then!"

"Y-you are – making me feel – shy," Arletta told him in a hesitant little voice.

"I adore you when you are shy."

As if he could wait no longer, he lifted her chin and his lips were on hers.

As he kissed her and the rapture within her heart began to leap up to her lips, she felt him undoing her gown.

A moment later it fell like a soft sigh to the ground.

He picked her up in his arms and carried her to the huge bed.

For a moment she did not really understand what was happening, she only felt a wild excitement sweep over her that seemed to be part of the beating of her heart.

And yet her love was more than that.

It was in her mind and in her soul and they belonged to the Duc.

He laid her down against the lace-trimmed pillows and drew the sheet over her.

Then, as the sunshine streaming in through the windows that overlooked the gardens and the fountains seemed to blind her eyes, he was beside her.

His arms were around her and she felt herself trembling with the wonder of it.

She knew that he too was feeling as if the angels were singing and already they had left the earth and were flying into the sky.

"*Je t'aime*! I love you!" the Duc sighed.

His lips were on hers and his hand was touching her body and she could feel his heart beating against hers.

"Teach – me. Oh, teach me about – love," she whispered.

Then she knew that there was no language on earth that they could express what they felt for each other in.

But there was no need for words.

Their love was life itself, the life that came from God and which was to be theirs for Eternity.

OTHER BOOKS IN THIS SERIES

The Barbara Cartland Eternal Collection is the unique opportunity to collect all five hundred of the timeless beautiful romantic novels written by the world's most celebrated and enduring romantic author.

Named the Eternal Collection because Barbara's inspiring stories of pure love, just the same as love itself, the books will be published on the internet at the rate of four titles per month until all five hundred are available.

The Eternal Collection, classic pure romance available worldwide for all time.

1. Elizabethan Lover
2. The Little Pretender
3. A Ghost in Monte Carlo
4. A Duel of Hearts
5. The Saint and the Sinner
6. The Penniless Peer
7. The Proud Princess
8. The Dare-Devil Duke
9. Diona and a Dalmatian
10. A Shaft of Sunlight
11. Lies for Love
12. Love and Lucia
13. Love and the Loathsome Leopard
14. Beauty or Brains
15. The Temptation of Torilla
16. The Goddess and the Gaiety Girl
17. Fragrant Flower
18. Look, Listen and Love
19. The Duke and the Preacher's Daughter
20. A Kiss For The King
21. The Mysterious Maid-Servant
22. Lucky Logan Finds Love
23. The Wings of Ecstasy
24. Mission to Monte Carlo
25. Revenge of the Heart
26. The Unbreakable Spell
27. Never Laugh at Love
28. Bride to a Brigand
29. Lucifer and the Angel
30. Journey to a Star
31. Solita and the Spies
32. The Chieftain without a Heart
33. No Escape from Love
34. Dollars for the Duke
35. Pure and Untouched
36. Secrets
37. Fire in the Blood
38. Love, Lies and Marriage
39. The Ghost who fell in love
40. Hungry for Love
41. The wild cry of love
42. The blue eyed witch
43. The Punishment of a Vixen
44. The Secret of the Glen
45. Bride to The King
46. For All Eternity

47. A King in Love
48. A Marriage Made in Heaven
49. Who Can Deny Love?
50. Riding to The Moon
51. Wish for Love
52. Dancing on a Rainbow
53. Gypsy Magic
54. Love in the Clouds
55. Count the Stars
56. White Lilac
57. Too Precious to Lose
58. The Devil Defeated
59. An Angel Runs Away
60. The Duchess Disappeared
61. The Pretty Horse-breakers
62. The Prisoner of Love
63. Ola and the Sea Wolf
64. The Castle made for Love
65. A Heart is Stolen
66. The Love Pirate
67. As Eagles Fly
68. The Magic of Love
69. Love Leaves at Midnight
70. A Witch's Spell
71. Love Comes West
72. The Impetuous Duchess
73. A Tangled Web
74. Love Lifts the Curse
75. Saved By A Saint
76. Love is Dangerous
77. The Poor Governess
78. The Peril and the Prince
79. A Very Unusual Wife
80. Say Yes Samantha
81. Punished with love
82. A Royal Rebuke
83. The Husband Hunters
84. Signpost To Love
85. Love Forbidden
86. Gift of the Gods
87. The Outrageous Lady
88. The Slaves of Love
89. The Disgraceful Duke
90. The Unwanted Wedding
91. Lord Ravenscar's Revenge
92. From Hate to Love
93. A Very Naughty Angel
94. The Innocent Imposter
95. A Rebel Princess
96. A Wish Come True
97. Haunted
98. Passions In The Sand
99. Little White Doves of Love
100. A Portrait of Love
101. The Enchanted Waltz
102. Alone and Afraid
103. The Call of the Highlands
104. The Glittering Lights
105. An Angel in Hell
106. Only a Dream
107. A Nightingale Sang
108. Pride and the Poor Princess
109. Stars in my Heart
110. The Fire of Love
111. A Dream from the Night
112. Sweet Enchantress
113. The Kiss of the Devil
114. Fascination in France
115. Love Runs in
116. Lost Enchantment
117. Love is Innocent
118. The Love Trap
119. No Darkness for Love
120. Kiss from a Stranger
121. The Flame Is Love
122. A Touch Of Love
123. The Dangerous Dandy
124. In Love In Lucca
125. The Karma of Love
126. Magic from the Heart
127. Paradise Found
128. Only Love
129. A Duel with Destiny
130. The Heart of the Clan

131. The Ruthless Rake
132. Revenge Is Sweet
133. Fire on the Snow
134. A Revolution of Love
135. Love at the Helm
136. Listen to Love
137. Love Casts out Fear
138. The Devilish Deception
139. Riding in the Sky
140. The Wonderful Dream
141. This Time it's Love
142. The River of Love
143. A Gentleman in Love
144. The Island of Love
145. Miracle for a Madonna
146. The Storms of Love
147. The Prince and the Pekingese
148. The Golden Cage
149. Theresa and a Tiger
150. The Goddess of Love
151. Alone in Paris
152. The Earl Rings a Belle
153. The Runaway Heart
154. From Hell to Heaven
155. Love in the Ruins
156. Crowned with Love
157. Love is a Maze
158. Hidden by Love
159. Love Is The Key
160. A Miracle In Music
161. The Race For Love
162. Call of The Heart
163. The Curse of the Clan
164. Saved by Love
165. The Tears of Love
166. Winged Magic
167. Born of Love
168. Love Holds the Cards
169. A Chieftain Finds Love
170. The Horizons of Love
171. The Marquis Wins
172. A Duke in Danger
173. Warned by a Ghost
174. Forced to Marry
175. Sweet Adventure
176. Love is a Gamble
177. Love on the Wind
178. Looking for Love
179. Love is the Enemy
180. The Passion and the Flower
181. The Reluctant Bride
182. Safe in Paradise
183. The Temple of Love
184. Love at First Sight
185. The Scots Never Forget
186. The Golden Gondola
187. No Time for Love
188. Love in the Moon
189. A Hazard of Hearts
190. Just Fate
191. The Kiss of Paris
192. Little Tongues of Fire
193. Love under Fire
194. The Magnificent Marriage
195. Moon over Eden
196. The Dream and The Glory
197. A Victory for Love
198. A Princess in Distress
199. A Gamble with Hearts
200. Love strikes a Devil
201. In the arms of Love
202. Love in the Dark
203. Love Wins
204. The Marquis Who Hated Women
205. Love is Invincible
206. Love Climbs in
207. The Queen Saves the King
208. The Duke Comes Home